"Harold Myra writes often about integrity, compassion, and grace. Now he rekindles the spirit of Screwtape to show how those gospel values are subverted by our anxieties, distrust, politics, and self-interest. With sincerity and satire, this tale helps us escape the whispers and listen to the words of hope."

—MARK SARGENT
Westmont College

"Harold Myra is one of the most versatile Christian authors of our generation. For over fifty years readers have enjoyed his wide range of styles, from fantasy and children's books, to devotionals, biography, and leadership. Myra's *Whispers From The Dark Side* brings the classic *Screwtape Letters* to life for a new generation."

—KEITH STONEHOCKER
Executive VP (retired), *Christianity Today*

"Harold Myra, drawing on decades of leadership in Christian publishing, has created a mythic novel that alerts readers to subtle whispers inching us toward the dark side. It's a page-turner story. One we might wisely recall at moments of subtle temptation."

—CAROLYN NYSTROM
Author of *What Happens When We Die?*

"When a wise saint like Harold Myra dives into the *Screwtape Letters* genre, it's worth paying attention. With his characteristically direct and devotional style, Myra confronts false cultural dichotomies and celebrates the missional power of prayer. This quirky little book packs a helpful and hopeful punch, left and right."

—DANIEL J. TREIER
Wheaton College Graduate School

"Just how does the devil organize his team to mess up our world, our personal lives? We don't know precisely . . . but Harold Myra has a pretty good guess. With a fertile imagination and great story-telling ability he pulls back the smoky curtain to show what's *really* going on. Thank you, Harold, for the heads-up."

—DEAN MERRILL
Author of *Sinners in the Hands of an Angry Church*

"An entertaining story of romance, temptation, unfulfilled dreams, power. Let your imagination dig a little deeper with Harold Myra and recognize a subtle but hostile spiritual world intent on re-straining good and strangling the unwary. These days, *Whispers* is a particularly good read when you don't know where the next surprise will strike."

—TED PAMPEYAN
Minister

"The battle for our souls is a cosmic battle, yet one that touches the most vulnerable places in each of our lives. Harold Myra writes perceptively as one who knows keenly the culture around us and as one who has steadily brought the light to dark places through his life and his writing."

—CAROL SAVAGE PLUEDDEMANN
Retired SIM missionary and Minister of Congregational Life,
Immanuel Presbyterian Church, Warrenville, Illinois

"Are we really surrounded by an invisible world in which demons and angels battle for the souls of mankind? Harold Myra, drawing on all of his skills as a great writer, has given us a deeply imagined answer to this ancient question. The answer is terrifying. And filled with hope."

—JACK MODESETT
Houston businessman

WHISPERS FROM THE DARK SIDE

Harold Myra

WHISPERS FROM
THE DARK SIDE

A Devilish Tale
of Seduction and Grace

CASCADE *Books* • Eugene, Oregon

WHISPERS FROM THE DARK SIDE
A Devilish Tale of Seduction and Grace

Cascade Books
An Imprint of Wipf and Stock Publishers
199 W. 8th Ave., Suite 3
Eugene, OR 97401

www.wipfandstock.com

PAPERBACK ISBN: 978-1-7252-5282-0
HARDCOVER ISBN: 978-1-7252-5283-7
EBOOK ISBN: 978-1-7252-5284-4

Cataloguing-in-Publication data:

Names: Myra, Harold, author.
Title: Whispers from the dark side : a devilish tale of seduction and grace / Harold Myra.
Description: Eugene, OR: Cascade Books, 2020
Identifiers: ISBN 978-1-7252-5282-0 (paperback) | ISBN 978-1-7252-5283-7 (hardcover) | ISBN 978-1-7252-5284-4 (ebook)
Subjects: LCSH: Devil—Christianity. | Spiritual life—Christianity.
Classification: BT982 .M95 2020 (print) | BT982 (ebook)

Manufactured in the U.S.A.   JUNE 17, 2020

PART ONE

THE SOURCE

Aliens.

Are they out there somewhere? Are they among us?

Movies, documentaries, literature, and folk tales depict sentient beings impinging on our world, including angels and demons. How much is imagination and speculation? How much is somehow real and at the core of the human condition?

When thousands of strange messages suddenly appeared on a startled secretary's computer in East Orange, New Jersey, government officials investigating suspected a hoax. However, as code-breakers and linguists studied them, they began to conclude the odd verbiage was not of human invention.

To avoid conspiracy theories and wild conjecture, the government made plans to inform the public. Our company was hired to edit the raw translations into accessible English.

Scholars interpreting the messages found them disturbing . . . and so did our editorial team. Our job, though, was to package them for readers—to capture for general release the meanings, tone, and sharp edges of these troubling transmissions.

Yet how could we translate the abundance of prurient accusations, scatological asides, and nearly indecipherable references? Some on our team grimaced, held their noses, and declared the project too vile and disgusting to complete.

But there was a story in there, mixed among the multiple threads and threatening rants . . . a story of a young man, a young woman, a college community, and the deadly results of diabolical whispers. We kept at it, digging for core meanings, selecting English idioms, and deleting messages unrelated to the emerging narrative.

Packaging the story—to make it readable and comprehensible—challenged the most creative among us. We finally decided to group the messages into ten sections. For each grouping we studied the raw translations and freely chose words and phrases to convey the meanings for a wide range of readers. We then created headings and titles drawn from the messages.

One editor suggested readers would profit from outside references. We decided to include selected quotations about evil spirits active in human affairs, placing them as "intermissions" to relieve toxic-message fatigue.

During the editing process, our team's widely varied opinions made for lively debate. Some believed the East Orange download might be a bizarre electronic hoax; others thought it was authentically alien.

We invite readers to come to their own conclusions.

># I <

THE BOY IN THE BASEMENT

∧∧∧∧∧∧

"You are not there to inflict pain, nor to enjoy it.
You are there to snare his soul."

∧∧∧∧∧∧∧

Bookstore Skirmish

Gnatsplat,

What's the matter with you, sending me a message that when the young woman smiled at your client in that bookstore it was "no big deal"?

No big deal? You muck-brained idiot! You knew she was dangerous. And your boy smiled back at her!

You should have lured his eyes elsewhere, but you were either snoozing or stupid—or both.

A week ago you were given a dossier on that woman's vigorous faith, so how could you ignore her smiling at him? What do they teach you little demons these days? There she was, just an aisle away from him in the stacks, and you were oblivious.

I've seen the clip. You had your man drenched in self-pity, looking at luxury-car magazines, but you were so absorbed enjoying his miseries, you never noticed the woman coming. This little Miss Prissy could contaminate everything you've gotten into him!

When she noticed him and smiled, did you instantly fuel the young man's resentments of privileged women? No.

Did you suck him back into his self-pity? Into those luxury cars beyond his reach? No again. You let him smile back.

Let me remind you that a woman like her, saturated with the Enemy's presence and protections, cannot be manipulated the ways you manipulate your man.

This is a much trickier game, Gnatsplat, than you know how to play.

Devious Master, but I was aware and totally alert. I was whispering to him about exactly that—his self-pity and resentments—but she came around the corner suddenly, and I tried—

Stop sniveling, Gnatsplat!

You let it happen. You knew the Enemy's hold on the woman. For years your incompetent colleagues have whispered, taunted, lured, and humiliated her, but nothing has pulled her toward us.

How long will we put up with you and the dimwit tempters you hang out with? Most of you imps woolgather through your warfare classes and they graduate you anyway. You then blunder around on the battlefields and lose skirmish after skirmish.

You remind me of those idiotic demons Jesus sent into a herd of pigs—just the right place for them, actually . . . shown by their running into a lake and drowning.

You know the pig story, but you don't learn. You bask in the glow of our success in this culture—you're euphoric about the spread of rage and the crushing of civility. But we were doing all the heavy lifting on that long before you came along.

Beware, Gnatsplat. Can you smell a different herd of swine eager for you?

Wake up. Lure the soul of this young man—that's your only job.

DO THIS:

Feed his bitterness at his father's deserting him. Thanks to us, he's one of millions now fatherless and aimless.

Make him brood about having to live in his mother's leaky basement with the spiders he hates. Feed his fears of feeling

7

yet another spider crawling in his sheets or across his nostrils. Exploit his mother's laughing at his fears, and inflame his anger at the latest man in her life who shares her bed.

Make him feel defeated by his job failures and low grades in his college courses.

Above all, keep him away from that woman. You've admitted he now hopes to see her in their speech class tomorrow. Make him resent her, as he's resented all young women with money, drive, and connections. Bring back memories of that saucy art major who flirted and made promises, then dropped him.

Yesterday we noticed how amused you were as your boy was frantically flailing at his hair with the spider in it. We, too, find his fears amusing. Maybe we should call him Spiderboy. The name has a fitting ring to it, don't you think?

Spiderboy—oblivious to our sticky strands all over him . . . a Spiderboy with no super powers at all.

But Basement Boy will do. He's your boy to tend in the basement with all our allurements and fears. Be sure to keep his anger simmering. Suck him into all those dark mutterings you've so often whispered to him.

Remember, Gnatsplat, you are not there to inflict pain, nor to enjoy it—you are there to snare his soul.

The Helpless Woman

Sliptrip,

You've been working for months to seduce this young woman assigned to you, but what progress have you made? The answers are disturbing. She's still Miss Prissy Pure. You and

Gnatsplat and all of you addled imps are frittering away your opportunities.

Why can't you get through to this woman? Answer me!

Devious Master, believe me, I am working on her all the time, always looking for a way to wedge in even a whiff of rebellion. But she has this terrible, childish habit of confessing every trifle of a sin, and when she opens her palms in prayers of helplessness, those meddlers from the Enemy rush to her.

I'm always keeping before me a list of her petty sins, trying to gain some leverage, and I try and try and try to plant seeds of pride, hoping to grow them into arrogance and feeling superior to unbelievers, but she's full of that wretched humility that starves our seeds.

Her family is no better—what troubles they cause!

We know all about that. After her mother's death her father kept finding ways to "bring beauty out of grief." We were enraged at all the celebrations of that mother snatched from us—

—yes, yes, enraging, and everything I throw at my girl deepens her dependence on the Enemy, and whatever I whisper to her is countered by one of those quick-and-ready celestials, but I'm keeping at it all the time, honest I am, I really, really am . . .

You've never been honest, Sliptrip, so don't pretend to be now.

It's clear you have no effective plans to break through her defenses, let alone the protections around her.

You need subtle strategies. Don't let her suspect she's dealing with spiritual issues at all.

Get started:

THREE WAYS TO SEDUCE HER

First, fuel her dismay at the lack of marriageable men in her generation. Hit her where she's vulnerable—her bewilderment that her longings for a mate are always dashed. She wants a man like her father, but fortunately for us, she's unlikely to find one.

In this culture, we've thinned the herd of "good men" considerably.

Have her dwell on the day she was alone on the trail with the man she was starting to love. Intensify her disgust when she remembers catching him in his big lie and then seeing him smirk.

Stop letting her feel triumphant that she roughly shoved him off the trail and then strode away. No! Get swirling in your Miss Prissy a longing for sweet revenge. Keep her stewing on the man's lies.

Make her savor self-pity.

Try for bitter laughter as she remembers the expressions on his face.

Second, liberate her. Plant thoughts of how stifling her family and faith are . . . and things her father does to make her feel controlled. Knowing how protective fathers can be, you'll surely find resentments to stir up. After all, she's a young woman full of sexual and survival drives.

Use her classmates to crack open her worldview. Select women with man-baggage, ones with abusive fathers or boyfriends. Find ones with our love/hate chaos churning.

Third, your patient's dossier indicates she has a temper. How sweet anger can be! Use it.

Unfortunately, her temper has been focused mainly as outrage about abused children. Her do-gooding in her community helps you not at all, but you can change that. Here's the stew you can brew:

>Shape her concerns for others into judging the bad guys, and that all bad guys must be punished. Give the bad guys a common identity—everyone who disagrees with her about social and political issues.

>As you will soon hear, one of our randy male professors has been identified as an abuser. Perfect! Have her join the inevitable campaign to expel and punish him. Fuel her rage, whispering repeatedly that her anger is righteous indignation.

>Sprinkle in specks of superior smugness that she's not evil like so many men.

Sliptrip, pull your Miss Prissy into what we're achieving these days! Everywhere tempters are giddy at seeing all the fresh hostility—outrage crackling like live wires loose in a storm.

Exploit the rage. I've seen the list of her friends, among them a feisty conservative and a radical progressive. Choose one and get your woman into one camp or the other.

Fuel her emotions.

Blur the complexities.

Have her absorb media that makes her despise the opposition.

Use your tools, Sliptrip! Stir her concerns into a stew with our time-tested ingredients: Sweet revenge. Love/hate chaos. Righteous indignation shaped into "holier than thou."

But don't think you can use Gnatsplat's young man to draw her into his emptiness. Keep those two apart.

Stop dawdling and start tempting. Remember: as with any soul, your woman is vulnerable.

———

Night Moves

Gnatsplat:

I'll reserve judgment on whether you did well to keep your Basement Boy at his video game so long he slept in and missed his class. It's helpful that it kept him from that dangerous woman, but be careful. You've told me he's been dwelling on the smile she gave him in the bookstore. Enemy agents will keep slipping such enticements into his mind . . . or, even more alarming for Sliptrip, a spark of interest from his Miss Prissy.

You know how adept those spirits are at using sexual attractions. Celestials are quick to celebrate human pleasures and their natural purposes, whispering about love and created wonders and how humans should be grateful to their Maker, happy to be alive.

Stifle all that!

Stick to our formula: sex and more sex without commitment, more and more self, less and less pleasure.

We work at such distinct disadvantages since we didn't create these minds and bodies. All we can do is distort the natural.

It's all so rotten! Why are we—

—Don't whine! Just inject contaminants into their celebrations. And stay alert. Souls well hooked like your young man too often break loose.

The "Fortunate Event"

Gnatsplat:

What a splendid moment this morning! When your Basement Boy came into class late, sheepish from ditching the previous class, and when he saw the professor slowly arch her eyebrows—

—Devious Master, not to interrupt, but I'm so glad you noticed, and I helped make everything happen, I was whispering to him all that morning about how unfair everything was and how women now have all the advantages and the speech class is stupid and the college is ripping him off so it all was perfect for when he walked in and the professor glared at him—

Shut up, Gnatsplat! You and all the tempters involved are clamoring for the credit. If anyone should be glowing right now, it's Tumbletwit. He's been grooming this professor for years, seasoning all her memories with resentments.

We've been watching the replay. Your boy had no idea she would—

—Exactly! My guy was bewildered and flustered, and the professor loved watching his reactions. Who would have thought we could entice her to—

Not "we." It was that frizzy old imp Tumbletwit who enticed her! When your Basement Boy first enrolled in her class, he saw a chance to draw his professor into the pleasure of humiliating a male. The moment she noticed his name on her class list, Tumbletwit whispered to her, "Think about this boy. What if you assigned him to make a speech against male hegemony?"

Imagine that, Gnatsplat. Male hegemony! This young man with a confused male identity, living in his mother's basement with no power, no future, and most of all, no mentor or direction in life, would be required to denounce male hegemony, about which he understood nothing.

But Tumbletwit did, wise old fiend. He had been observing his professor's gender research for years and he knew the idea would intrigue her. He let it percolate in her mind.

Later he added the twist: the boy should address Gloria Steinem's quip that a woman without a man is like a fish without a bicycle. His speech title would be, "Does a Woman Need a Man?"

His professor couldn't stop smiling every time she thought about it. And then Tumbletwit came up with his very best bit. He suggested your boy would have to speak not in his own voice but in the person of Gloria Steinem.

Yes, and how sweet it was to watch his reactions as she told him what he had to do. As his eyes were tightening, the professor stared at him with that glare in her eyes we love to see.

. . . the glare with her flat, ambiguous smile . . . our kind of smile.

We pretty much own this professor now—but it took years to get her breathing our exhalations. Isn't it fascinating how the highly literate succumb? As a child and young adult, she resisted our whispers. But then her growing hatred for her philandering husband year after year slowly wore that away.

After she divorced him, earned her PhD, and shacked up with our randy literature professor—only to be dumped by him—she began listening more and more to Tumbletwit. He filled her with our vapors, making academic achievement her god.

Everyone worships something . . . and we've lured her onto an endless chase to be smarter than the smartest—going faster and faster on our hamster wheel, gulping pills to maintain the pace. Sometimes this erudite woman can be an anxious mess.

That's why we call her our Ms. Sourbelly.

Sour she is! My guy makes lousy grades, but he isn't stupid—he sensed her hostility when she started telling him—

—Hostility born of nasty moments with men . . . but Tumbletwit has always been careful to feed her the right kind of rage. It's a fine line.

The Enemy uses rage for his own purposes . . . but it's our brand of hatreds and revenge that keeps this world spinning and souls tumbling our way.

The Enemy's brand of rage is pie in the sky: to promote justice and peace and (*gag*) love so that "the Father's will be done on earth as it is in heaven."

Good luck with that! This is our world.

It's so obvious. Jesus admitted it's our world when he didn't contradict Our Father Below when he offered him powers if he'd fall down and worship. His rebel believers sing it's *their* Father's world, but look around. Insurrections and warfare everywhere, rapes, religious atrocities, sex trafficking, genocides . . . it's ours, all ours . . .

Gnatsplat, you're on the winning side in this war! So act like a winner.

Yes, Devious Master, I've successfully tempted my client to—

Oh, just shut up and enjoy watching this morning's clips. I am!

Who says we tempters are humorless? When we saw her bragging to other faculty members this afternoon that she gave the Gloria Steinem assignment "for the boy's own good—to sensitize him," it generated enormously satisfying laughter down here.

⌒

Failure to Grin

Sliptrip,

Some of us here think you may be in over your head with your prissy young woman. This morning when our Ms. Sourbelly assigned our Basement Boy to speak as Steinem, and the rest of the class was grinning, your girl watched stiff-faced, sober as a judge.

That's a problem—your problem.

Unlike most of her classmates, your girl keeps resisting the cynicism we've salted into this culture. She actually cringed at her professor's tone.

Yes, when she saw the boy wince. It made her remember his smile at the bookstore and that made her hate his being ridiculed and—

—and much worse than that, her empathy extends to everybody!

Sliptrip, salt in some realism. Humans can be loathsome. Help her imagine what she should do to loathsome creatures.

Man/Woman Websites

Gnatsplat,

Now that your boy is fed up with the speech class, reinforce his decision to drop it. Use his humiliating experience to deepen his self-pity.

Yes, Devious Master, that's just what I'm doing—reminding him that everything bad happens to him . . . spiders . . . nasty girls . . . his mother's latest man he detests . . .

Keep blending his self-pity with anger. Remember this: the skilled tempter's trick is to blend the scrabble for one's rights differently for men and for women. What a delight it is to visit male websites that bash women, and to visit female websites that bash men!

Wars have limitations, driving the desperate into the arms of the Enemy. But war between the sexes is our kind of jazz. It resonates far deeper than these creatures realize . . . their identities float . . . and if we're clever, they float right toward us.

Properly tended, your boy's assignment will further degrade his respect for women. But not for his mother! We want him to identify with her and to wallow in his mother's miseries. We want him to blame everything bad on his absent father.

Some day we may change strategies and have him feel contempt for his mother, but not now. As he sees her spiraling downward from overwork at her dead-end jobs, her loss of friends, and all the betrayals by the men who come and go, let him fully identify with her.

His mother hates her life, and well she should. The nearby church would readily help her, but she doesn't think so. We had a strong hand, of course, in firming up her conviction that all church people are judgmental and that if she ever entered the church she walks by, she'd be humiliated.

Feed his feelings of impotence about all that. Remind him of the times his mother rebuffed him when he tried to get her to change her ways.

And, Gnatsplat, make sure he has no intention of going back to that class where Sliptrip's woman might smile at him again.

>2<

SPARKS AT STARBUCKS

^^^^^^

"The worst sort of laughter.
Laughter as odious as a fervent prayer."

^^^^^^^

———

Squelch His Euphoria

Gnatsplat,

I hate Calvin and Hobbes!

How could you let your man and that woman meet like that? I saw everything—watched our replays the instant I heard about it. There he was in the college bookstore, his eyes on the pages of *Something Under the Bed Is Drooling,* an infuriating book like all the other Calvin and Hobbes tripe.

Why do I hate that six-year-old pagan? Let me count the ways.

Yes, Calvin is full of just the sort of original sin we count on. The boy creates misery and confusion everywhere—his self-centeredness is great grist for tempters. But the strip is subversive. We're exposed by it, and ridiculed. And you, naïve little fiend, probably had no idea that human laughter is so often used by the Enemy.

Worst of all, the boy's stuffed animal Hobbes—the tiger with insights from above—always has the last word.

Bad stuff!

And then, in that bookstore, with your man engrossed in the book and laughing, that same dangerous woman—Slip-trip's woman who smiled at him, the Miss Prissy I've warned you about!—she sees him and walks over to him, sticks her nose above the book and starts laughing, too. The worst sort of laughter!

Laughter full of good spirits.

Laughter from the pit of Paradise.

Laughter as odious as a fervent prayer.

Was their meeting a mere "coincidence"? Hardly! Those simpering-sweet spirits who keep butting in barely conceal their brazen coincidences—this was all their doing.

I told you this woman is dangerous. You should have kept your man out of that bookstore and never have let him see *Something Under the Bed*.

Get busy! Squelch his euphoria about laughing with her. Sneak in thoughts she's actually mocking his juvenile interests. Don't let him savor their jabbering about Calvin and his tiger. Keep him occupied in his basement and pull a few coincidences of your own.

Keep these two apart.

I'm told by Sliptrip the woman is not attracted to your Basement Boy, she's just infected with a bad case of compassion. She thought their professor's Steinem assignment was demeaning, and she actually considered confronting our Ms. Sourbelly, and then she felt guilty she hadn't. Seeing him in the store, she went right to him.

Sliptrip claims he's working hard to keep his girl from your boy.

Don't believe it, Gnatsplat.

I don't, Master, I don't, and when I jerked his chain about it, Sliptrip belched out that I was misbegotten horse drench—

—Well, you are horse drench, Gnatsplat, you are! And I watched you belch back at him that he should stuff his snout in puke and corpse worms. You imbecile imps can squabble and squeal all you want, but don't cry to me when they come for you and drag you—

—Oh, Master, I only confronted him to make him follow through on what you have been telling us and I was only—

Stop fawning! Shut up and get to work.

Calvin and Hobbes is stealthy stuff, but you can infect your man's enthusiasm. Make him identify with the narcissistic little boy—never with his insidious tiger Hobbes.

Your man thinks of himself as the center of the universe. Never let that change.

———

Lies and Excuses

Sliptrip,

You're desperate to involve your woman with Gnatsplat's boy, but that's not the plan! Your last message gave the impression—

—Yes, Devious Master, yes, I was seeing those possibilities, but I had nothing at all to do with their meeting in that bookstore, and I assure you I am sticking to our strategy, for I always obey all commands—

Of course you do. You're incompetent, but you're not a complete idiot.

Pay attention, Sliptrip, because the infernal powers below are tired of your excuses. We must have results. Now!

Yes, I understand, Master, really, really I do, and I've used all the enticements and spins recommended, but she's attending a Sunday class in her church taught by a retired anthropology professor—an anthropology professor! This old woman is a menace.

In her eighties she still travels all over the world, adapting the dangerous parts of religions into her worldview—and worst of all, her worldview is saturated with Scriptures.

This old female agitator is full of stories of persecuted villagers and refugees finding faith and she keeps exposing us, and my girl is soaking it all in. She barely hears me anymore.

You dribbling pig's snout! Your battlefield ignorance is blind siding you.

We're at war. Wake up.

As for this anthropology professor, we've been trying to control her for a long, long time. When her first marriage failed, we thought she was easy pickings, but that's when the Enemy recruited her, and she's been fighting us ever since. Again and again we've battered her and broken down her defenses, but she falls on her knees and confesses and weeps and rises to do more mischief.

The imps tempting her grumble and spit and call her Mrs. Gollyglowworm. She has way too much spiritual alacrity. When she gets hit hard, she prays—then skitters off to a concert or the library or to help somebody. Our legions keep whispering to her how useless her prayers are, but she's so saturated with the Scriptures and the Enemy's Spirit that even though her old body is shutting down, she forces herself to keep getting things done.

It's disgusting how often she oozes into that insufferable giddiness she calls joy.

Exactly! Exactly! And instead of divine wrath she emphasizes in her classes that the Enemy loves these vermin! Plus those celestials are butting in all the time telling my young, impressionable woman it's true, all true, that they are loved by the One who made them, just as this old woman is saying, and—

—Of course it's all true, Sliptrip! Of course the Enemy loves them. That's their whole story. It's the root of their lamentable tale.

You've always known that. We don't spend all those hours studying their Book to refute the idea. We study the thing to look for loopholes, to demolish, to sow doubt, to subvert.

But how can I subvert my girl if she won't listen to me?

Persist! Get your Miss Prissy absorbed on her phone to drown out the anthropologist's rebel-talk. Heighten her anxieties about what she sees on her screens. Sow doubts about the Scriptures.

I suspect the holy-writ classes you took are now mere background noise in your mushy brain. Review your notes. Know their Book. Study the way Our Father Below used Scriptures to tempt our Enemy in the wilderness.

Let me repeat: your woman is contagious. Keep her away from Gnatsplat's boy.

———

Basement Bliss

Gnatsplat,

Why is it you always send me bad news? And why did you fail to tell me that while they were still in the store, Miss Prissy purchased that damnable *Something Under the Bed Is Drooling* and put it in his hand?

Now you say he's in his basement studying it like he's never studied anything before, and he bursts out laughing?

Your report is infuriating. Don't you dare let your man come out of his cave with a smile on his face.

———

Ruinous Spunk and Empathy

Sliptrip,

You rancid scrap of rat bait—the lowerarchy is aghast at this morning's incident with your Miss Prissy and Tumbletwit's professor. Now we'll both be watched from below!

Why didn't you do something—anything—to stop that debacle? Believe me, I won't protect you from the consequences—

—But, Master, who would suspect young women would stick up for a boy they barely know? Those same girls were grinning at him when he was stunned at hearing about Steinem—

—Don't play stupid with me, Sliptrip. You know exactly how your woman recruited those girls and how they confronted Tumbletwit's professor. You let it happen. Your Miss Prissy picked two Midwest classmates who didn't like Steinem one bit and a third who'd been wounded by Sourbelly's sarcasm. She then flipped the boy's assignment into a justice issue.

But I tried—

—You tried nothing that worked. You were dumbfounded as she recruited those classmates. And later, outside Sourbelly's office, you watched like a stone gargoyle while Miss Prissy pep-talked the three girls and then stepped into her professor's office full of spunk and empathy.

A ruinous concoction—your Miss Prissy's spunk and empathy.

The last thing we want is a gaggle of heroic women standing up for a humiliated young man.

Of course, of course, and these days that never happens, that just never happens! So how was I to know—

—You should have stifled your woman's empathy for Gnatsplat's boy. Why did you let her get the idea she should stand up for him? You let her feelings fester into the ugly pustule of doing something. And you underestimated your girl. She had the brains to realize she could recruit those three classmates—

Yes, Devious Master, yes, but those Enemy spirits—

—You knew your client was listening to them! That's what ramped up her passion to right a wrong. And why are you complaining she had help from the other side? What did you expect? The celestials are always crusading against their view of injustice.

But there are so many of them and they come at the worst times, just when we have our humans dangling—

You screwed up, Sliptrip . . . and there's plenty of guilt to go around. Your fellow bumbler Tumbletwit was far too smug about having his woman under control. When those students demanded she change the boy's assignment, and when his Ms. Sourbelly with the deadly tongue caved in to their demand, he was stunned. And even though he'd long been sharpening his professor's verbal vitriol, he even failed to have her zing them with a tart retort as the students left.

Imagine his ineptitude!

It's true, it's true, Tumbletwit screwed up completely and—

—and nothing. That imp's failure helps you not one bit—you're up to your nose, Sliptrip, in sulfurous muck. Next thing you know, your Miss Prissy will seal her triumph over her professor by going to Gnatsplat's boy to tell him he can speak on any subject. Who knows what that will lead to?

Nothing good for us, I assure you.

Our Lecherous Professor

Tumbletwit,

Stop cowering!

You failed when Sliptrip's girl and her classmates confronted your professor about the boy's assignment. You failed to even have her zing those girls . . . and we keep account of all your blunders.

Despite that, you are to stay at your post. You've been basting your professor in our juices for a long, long time, keeping her furious at the way our poetry prof promised her love forever, then dumped her. We've observed your stirring up her rage when she sees him on campus, puffing on his pipe like a suffering poet, chatting up the girls.

Yes, Master, and as she's watched him across the room in faculty meetings, with his paunch growing more each year and his face starting to sag, she responds marvelously to my whispers of disgust.

And revenge! Get her in a vengeful mood. Have her hatch clever ways to make him suffer for what he did to her . . . and let those fantasies bleed into ideas about getting back at those students who confronted her.

>3<

SOMETHING
SUPERNATURAL

^^^^^^^

"Push her prayers toward an irresistible desire to
call down on the professor's head fire from heaven."

^^^^^^^^

Sneaky Angels

Gnatsplat:

What a bad week! Didn't I warn you those meddling spirits were up to something? How else did all this happen—Sliptrip's woman calling your man to tell him his speech assignment was changed and then, the very next day, their seeing each other at Starbucks?

A coincidence? Not really.

When you're playing hardball against these "ministering spirits," scramble! Block them.

You asked why I made such a big deal about Calvin and Hobbes. Let me sketch reality. You're aware, I'm sure, of the artwork on human greeting cards showing an angel on one shoulder and a demon on the other. We love it when they trivialize us—assuming we're figments of imagination. Yet those enemy angels on shoulders are sneaky. They use everything from light stuff like *Peanuts* and *Calvin and Hobbes* to tales like *The Brothers Karamazov*. You never know how they'll use what they call truth and beauty to pierce these eternal souls with their antiseptic light.

Your priority now is to keep your man away from that college campus. Don't let Sliptrip's young woman with her damnable cheeriness give him ideas for his speech.

Get him grumbling about the "stupid assignment." Make him feel hopeless about it.

Yes, I've been working hard at that, and I've been using all the excellent suggestions you've been sending me, and I successfully got him to spend half the night staring at some of our best bits on his old device and—

—Good. Keep him in his cave.

As his eyes flit across his screens, feed him doses of anxiety about terrorists and hurricanes and his student debt. Fuel his disdain for those who hate his worldview—a quite satisfactory one by the way: vague and uninformed, yet rigid about who is at fault and what should be done to them.

You want him numb, angry, and resenting everything, including his mother's boyfriend.

Remember, nothing matters but this: Will he surrender to us, or will he surrender to them?

—

Retaliation

Sliptrip:

You say your woman is praying for Tumbletwit's professor? Praying for someone she viscerally dislikes?

You wretched idiot! Your blasé attitude strikes me as serious negligence. Did you hear a strange, grinding noise in the night? Did you find it disturbing? You should! It was my teeth on edge, mixed with snarls from below at this most perilous of pieties. Don't you know that kind of selfless prayer is a triple threat:

First, it takes her beyond "give-me-and-bless-me" prayers to prayers that can shake our foundations.

Second, it gives those celestials hovering over her an excuse to barge into our territory and rattle that classroom.

Third, that kind of prayer hands the Enemy openings to disrupt Tumbletwit's work on his professor. Believe me, you will be held accountable for blunders that sabotage other imps' progress. Everywhere in this world is contested territory, and you must never, ever give celestials an opening to the clients we're tending.

You know how often we discover, when someone turns against us, that some unknown soul has been "interceding." Our prey suddenly sees our pleasures and freedoms as pits and webs.

Surely, from your classes on this disagreeable subject of intercessory prayer, you remember what happened with Augustine's mother. Here we had her son ensnared and entangled, but she prayed incessantly for him . . . yet the tempters back then didn't take it seriously. If we had known the consequences, we would have sent legions of tempters. Her son was ours, but because of her prayers, we lost him.

We've been dealing ever since with Augustine's mixed bag of interferences.

Thank you, Devious Master, for taking the time to instruct me, and I assure you I am not blasé about this crisis at all for I have been suggesting to my intransigent Miss Prissy all of the subtleties you've mentioned and all that I see in our manuals, and I'll keep at it night and day and—

—We shall see, Sliptrip, how effective you are, but here's how much trouble you're in. Unlike Augustine's mother interceding for the son she loved, your woman is doing something more difficult. She's obeying the Enemy's command to love one's enemies. That's a command humans can't handle without supernatural help.

That sort of obedience chills us.

Focus your efforts this way:

Worm your way into the prayers she's directing at this professor who is rightly ours. As she prays, guide her thoughts to the clever, biting sarcasm our Ms. Sourbelly uses on students. Have her take personal offense at every cutting remark.

Do anything to distract her from this incendiary praying for her "enemy."

Finally, have her judge her professor as so evil she's beyond her prayers. Persuade her to believe she is far more righteous than this bitter woman with the acerbic tongue. The goal is to push her prayers toward an irresistible desire to call down fire on the older woman's head.

Tumbletwit is working at producing a win-win for both you and him. He's intensifying his professor's rage at our libidinous lit prof who seduced her, and while he's doing that, he's spreading her fury to include your Miss Prissy.

Drucker and Kierkegaard

Gnatsplat,

When I told you to keep your man in his basement, you know very well I meant you should keep him escaping into his video games and porn and sleeping his days away. Don't you dare imply I bear any responsibility whatever for his sudden fascination with Starbucks. You were the one, you whimpering wretch, who let him meet the young woman there.

Yesterday in Starbucks you let his eyes linger on the cover of *It's Not About the Coffee,* and then you let him flip through its claims that Starbucks is all about team building. Gnatsplat, you have only yourself to blame for the surge in his chest about how he could become part of a team and his new eagerness to rise to challenges.

Apparently, they don't teach you ignorant imps about the ways so many management books denounce our world-wide leadership development.

The failures started decades ago when our tempters didn't keep Peter Drucker away from reading Kierkegaard. Drucker's conclusion that all humans are made in the Enemy's image made him a terrible choice to become the father of modern management. Now so many leadership books and conferences go on and on about empowering and energizing for the good of all.

They're dangerously tipped toward the light.

There are exceptions, of course. Ayn Rand can be helpful, especially in our cultivation of narcissists in our financial controls. But you need to take seriously the ways your man is awakening to visions dancing in his head. He's drawing from this Starbucks claptrap a growing sense of having a purpose in life.

If a man lives with purpose, we must constantly refine it.

So Sliptrip's Miss Prissy told your boy he's now free to choose his speech topic? Bad news! What could be worse than for him to preach employee empowerment with fire in his belly?

Double down on locking your man into the ruts you've worn into him. Don't forget, the Scriptures say men love darkness, and they love it more than the light.

Obviously! So, get his nose out of those seditious books and back into our basement temptations that have kept him with us for so long.

———

Retaliation Gone Awry

Tumbletwit,

Today you were hit by agitators from the Enemy, and you were sleeping at the switch.

Yes, you fueled your professor's rage and carefully guided her retaliation plan. She knew it was Miss Prissy who had talked her three classmates into confronting her, so ordering her to come alone to her office was a good start. It put your woman back in charge.

But listen up, Tumbletwit. What you ignored when Sliptrip's woman walked in was the energy field that came in with her.

She was all prayed up.

Didn't you realize her unseen allies were crowding in with her?

Your professor's glowering from behind her desk set the right tone, but you should have seen she overplayed her hand. Instead of slowly doling out her points, tightening the noose inch by inch, she fumbled when she saw the fire in Miss Prissy's eyes.

I've watched the clip from several angles. The young woman stood in front of the desk like a rooted tree. It was clear something strange was about to happen.

When your Ms. Sourbelly demanded, "Wipe the smile off your face," the smile did not change. It was not triumphal—not at all—and the girl's poise was beyond the natural. Her stance was precisely what we dread from young women!

Then, without a bit of sarcasm, she said, "I've been praying for you."

All of us watching that clip saw something supernatural pulsing and flowing over both of them.

Yes, Master, I didn't know what do and—

—You should have flashed into your professor distaste and disdain for the syrupy goodness coming at and over her. Your Ms. Sourbelly stood there like a child watching a movie.

And so did you.

You should have jolted her into cynicism. You should have made her feel the scene was like a cheap religious movie.

Yes, Master, I was doing just those things, but I seemed shrunk down, with no power whatever to communicate to her, and that lasted on and on . . . I was reduced to a mouse in the corner . . . reduced to squeaks unheard . . .

I heard your squeaks! As I watched the clip, I wanted to pinch your hairy little head.

Oh, Master, but now I'm getting through to my professor again, even though in all that craziness those meddling spirits got her thinking about her childhood and her parents long ago laughing with her and I know that's not good and—

—Tumbletwit, they're after her. Get your professor out of her childhood reveries. Focus on resentments at these students demeaning her.

Draw her back into the warm pleasures of vindictive fantasies of punishing our randy professor she loathes.

Go to the Brimstone site and immerse yourself in the section on using emotions to lure intellectuals.

PART TWO

INTERMISSION

It's time to take a short break from these messages.

Perhaps your reactions to them are similar to what one of our translators said—that working on the material made her feel as if she'd fallen into a dank sewer with rabid rats. She couldn't wait to get home and take a shower.

Others felt equally soiled. At the same time, all of us on the project marveled at the transmissions' sophistication. We had the unnerving sense that, considering human history and world conditions, these dark spirits' seductions have been highly successful.

That made us wonder how to comply with our government contract's stipulation that the product offered to the public must "in simple prose make the transmissions comprehensible, with relevant cultural references."

Which cultures? What references?

All cultures struggle with good and evil, gods and spirits, pranksters and trolls. References to the devil and evil could fill endless volumes—from ancient Scriptures to Dante's *Divine Comedy*, Goethe's *Faust*, and Milton's *Paradise Lost*, along with quips and comments from Martin Luther, Calvin, and C. S. Lewis . . . all sharply contrasted with writers rejecting traditional views of angels and demons.

We discussed how we could objectively choose references from the massive range of commentary on spirits active in human affairs. As we considered a great many, it became abundantly clear the more traditional quotations matched best with the download's illuminations of demonic ways and wiles.

Below you'll find our first set of related quotations.

<><><>

The devil's voice is sweet to hear.
—Stephen King

<><><>

It was pride that changed angels into devils.
—Saint Augustine

<><><>

The devil whispered, "It's pretty, but is it Art?"
—Rudyard Kipling

<><><>

You used to live in sin, just like the rest of the world, obeying the devil—the commander of the powers in the unseen world. He is the spirit at work in the hearts of those who refuse to obey God.
—Ephesians 2

<><><>

The devil has power to assume a pleasing shape.
—William Shakespeare

<><><>

Wherever God erects a house of prayer, the Devil always builds
a chapel there;
And 'twill be found, upon examination, the latter has the largest
congregation.
—Daniel Defoe

<><><>

Satan's successes are greatest when he has the name of God on
his lips.
—Mahatma Gandhi

<><><>

Satan will not outsmart us. We are familiar with his evil
schemes.
—2 Corinthians 2

<><><>

Jesus was led by the Spirit into the wilderness. . . . The devil took
him to the peak of a high mountain and showed him all the
kingdoms of the world and their glory. "I will give it all to you"
he said, "if you will kneel down and worship me." "Get out of
here, Satan," Jesus told him. "For the Scriptures say, 'You must
worship the Lord your God and serve only him.'" Then the devil
went away, and angels came and took care of Jesus.
—Mark 4

<><><>

When the angels arrive, the devils leave.
—Egyptian Proverb
<><><>

>4<

RINGS AND FLIES

∧∧∧∧∧∧

"Enemy fingerprints are all over *The Lord of the Rings*."

∧∧∧∧∧∧∧

———

A Woman Intrigued

Sliptrip,

So your Miss Prissy's interest in Gnatsplat's man spiked when he gave his Starbucks speech in the class. That's trouble.

I've viewed the scene. His delivery was far from polished, but his intensity got her attention. We view her piqued interest with alarm. Unfortunately, her compassion is edged with flickers of romantic interest.

Sliptrip, in this battle for her soul, you've failed to seed in even one significant contaminant. She not only keeps praying for Tumbletwit's professor—and, I might add, is praying for the young man—but she is on a spiritual peak. She will come down from that, of course. They always do.

Enemy spirits are rushing in to the young man because of his new readiness to learn. I am currently recruiting seasoned imps who owe me something to help Gnatsplat double down on manipulating his client.

I am also going to give a swift kick to Zitsit, her father's handler. Your woman's compassion sprouts from his constant consorting with the celestials.

Her father must be neutralized.

———

Incendiary Classics

Zitsit,

Don't expect to be mollycoddled any longer in your handling of this stubborn father. I've repeatedly warned you that seducing him would require skilled use of every bit of bait in the box.

Unfortunately, you've been dangling your lures like a novice.

You told me after his wife died that trying to crack open his faith was like striking a crowbar against granite. Zitsit, no one is impenetrable! Your man's trick is he keeps admitting his weaknesses to the Enemy. You've got to break that connection.

Make him believe his successes came from his own will-power—he does it his way, and he's "master of his fate."

That way, he'll do it our way.

You're playing a high-stakes game, Zitsit, with many souls in play. We're particularly concerned about his influence as a high school English teacher. We're doing extremely well with males these days, and you've got to knock him off his hobby horse of inspiring his teenage boys against us. His influence could spread, with disastrous results. Some busy-body journal-ist could come along and profile this gifted teacher contrast-ing *The Lord of the Rings* and *The Lord of the Flies* and their relevance to young men.

That's the last thing we want to go viral!

Yes, Master, his presentations are persuasive, but the boys don't pay attention to how they apply to them. All they care about are the dragons and sword fights and the grisly parts and—

—and you don't whiff the dangers, lazy imp? Listen up and I'll unpack them for you.

Millions have read these books and seen the movies, but most miss the meanings. We've numbed this culture to biologi-cal realities, but it's so obvious! Women need much less civiliz-ing. They want a faithful husband and most long to nurture babies. We're forced to subvert those instincts . . . but with men—ah, we have so many openings!

Although men also want to nest and nurture, they're mostly driven to spread their seed far and wide. Male biology urges: "Impregnate every attractive woman. Lust is natural! Enjoy! Make lots and lots of babies that are *your* babies."

That's biology. In that and countless other ways we count on uncivilized males to run the world—with us in charge. We want men disdaining women, inflicting pain on women and controlling them—not protecting and empowering them by the Enemy's playbook.

Girls can be mean, and women can be spiteful and useful, but boys and men *naturally* fit our strategies.

The books and movies of *The Lord of the Rings* unmask us and inspire males to resist our uses of them. Enemy fingerprints are all over it.

The Lord of the Flies shows what happens when no one civilizes boys. They end up worshipping a pig's head, descending into barbarity and murder.

Our kind of happy ending!

But we don't want people thinking about that. We don't want your teacher's *Rings* and *Flies* PowerPoint to get out beyond his classroom. Far be it from us to have to deal with boys who respond to celestial's urging them to break free of us and to rouse men in league with our Enemy.

You can thank Our Father Below that this culture is so busy empowering girls and women that very few notice what's happening to boys and men.

Yes, Devious Master, yes, and when he shows The Lord of the Flies *to his students, I keep whispering to him that these boys are no different from those schoolboys on the island, and these stupid boys in his classroom aren't worth his time. They're dead to his stories and they're dead to his prayers.*

Get real, Zitsit! We've seen from here that when he contrasts the heroism of *Rings* with the schoolboys' descent into barbarity in *Flies*, too many of his students get it. Dangerous realizations are now perking in their heads. Some are recognizing the dark side in their lives.

These boys are our boys! You've got to stop this, you slimy sluggard.

Yes, Devious Master, but—

—No excuses, just action! Sneak fresh temptations into this newly widowed man in his prime. He's vulnerable to one of our women. Make his needs and desires paramount.

Drain away all that empathy his daughter emulates. Heat up tensions between them.

Find creative ways to disconnect him from the Source.

———

The Fight in the Kitchen

Gnatsplat,

Crash scene! How satisfying.

After your setbacks of your boy's new energies and his successful speech, this latest is a marvelous change. The drama in his mother's kitchen last night was highly enjoyable to watch— three people knocked emotionally senseless by streams of blistering obscenities.

Now we assess the results. As I reviewed the clips, I made the following notes:

Little did your boy know that speaking up to protect his mother would trigger such savage reactions from the man in her life! Little did his mother's man know how viciously your boy would counter-attack! Best of all, little did any of them anticipate the devastation when the shouting was over.

The man knew his woman now hated him for attacking her son.

The son felt thrown out into darkness.

The mother was frozen.

You can take some credit for your work on this boy, but the other two handlers deserve even more for their years of cultivation. Your young client had no idea how tightly we had enmeshed his mother and her man in our webs.

He found out!

He thought his mother would love him for trying to stop her man from abusing her. Instead, she averted her eyes. When her man ordered her son to get out of the basement, and when both men started shouting, she became collateral damage.

All she could think of was how horrible it was they were yelling and threatening each other in her kitchen. She had no idea what damage she did to her son when she sided with the man against him. She was unaware of the implosion going on in her boy since we kept the same question reappearing in her head: "Why should I be caught between these two? Why don't they understand my hard, hard life? It's so unfair to me."

Unfair? Obviously! We work to arrange an unfair life for everybody.

Don't think our draining away her mother love was easy. When her boy was born, she was infected with plenty of it.

Mother love is a tough goodness to wear away, but we ground at it, like sand against skin. It may take a village to raise a child, but when her boy's father left, the village wasn't there for her.

But now, Gnatsplat, what's strategic is the state of your client. His identity was centered in his mother. Her rejection has cracked it wide open. Wounded in his core, he's more vulnerable than ever.

That's mostly very good for us. Yet since your prey is adrift, he's also vulnerable to other spirits.

Turmoil in identity puts souls in play.

Each human must decide one question: "Who is my Father? Whom will I forever obey?"

Let him keep hating his absent father . . . and now is the time to spread the hatred to his mother.

Clever Angling

Sliptrip,

Now that Gnatsplat's boy is on the street and your Miss Prissy wonders where he is—and as she comes down from her little triumph over Tumbletwit's professor—

—but, Devious Master, she's not coming down at all! You yourself said something unnatural happened in her office! My girl is still on a high that doesn't—

—Sliptrip, review Temptation 101. They always—*always!*—come down from peak spiritual experiences.

I know, I know . . . but she's so inspired and—

—Don't screw this up. Go to the Brimstone site that has everything you need to know about peaks-and-valleys temptations. Memorize the list of clever seductions categorized by spiritual highs, lows, and vulnerabilities.

Learn to use just the right bait. Select your lures like an old, savvy angler.

Get a hook in your prey.

———

Jail Euphoria

Gnatsplat,

Your glee at your boy's landing in jail because of a bar fight is unwarranted. Jail is never pure advantage for us.

Yes, I know—

—but you don't know! Everything you've been sending me this morning indicates you're just feeding on his despair and enjoying yourself. You don't even hint at the dangers when souls get imprisoned.

I'm aware of them, of course—

—then name them.

Well . . . I know . . . there have been . . .

. . . Your stammering says it all. You've forgotten the basics! Your man's more vulnerable in jail. Who knows what prison ministry or celestial whispers might hit him at just the wrong time?

Don't you remember your trainers telling you about Sol-zhenitsyn in the gulag? The Russian famously blathered, "Bless you, prison, bless you. Lying upon the rotting prison straw I came to realize that the object of life was not prosperity." We had the man ensnared in our systems, but when imprisoned, he responded to the celestials.

They're everywhere butting in. Solzhenitsyn served the Enemy for decades, causing us no end of trouble.

Look at the statistics on the Brimstone site showing the thousands of prisoners on this wretched planet who are, to use their obnoxious phrase, "headed for glory."

Wake up.

Your boy will be released soon, so while he's still in his cell, deepen his hatred for his father, step-fathers, and, now especially, his mother who betrayed him.

Remember, anyone who hates his mother is prime prey. As you would know if you'd kept up with your studies, we have millions of prisoners who hate their fathers, but almost none who hate their mothers.

This is your rare opportunity! Wrap your sticky strands around him tighter and tighter. Keep him dwelling day and night on the calamitous clash when his mother chose her man over him.

Be vigilant. You have him now, but no matter how many strands of habit you wrap around him, the Enemy is always waiting and ready to open a door . . .

>5<

BEAUTY AND THE BEAST

∧∧∧∧∧∧

"Trundle into his mind what he learned about
divine instructions to burn heretics and start holy wars."

∧∧∧∧∧∧∧

The Lost-Soul Meet-Up

Gnatsplat and Sliptrip,

Get your stories straight, you two inept pukeheads. You're so intent on blaming each other that you're screeching like bilious babies. Both of you were to keep your clients apart, but you failed miserably.

Just look at the clips.

Look at the clips!

Your boy, Gnatsplat, is a lost soul wandering onto the campus, stung from being locked in jail and now living in a drafty old attic with only a lone light bulb. Did you divert him from that campus? No. You didn't even stoke his resentments and fears he didn't belong in college.

Sliptrip, when your prissy girl noticed him on the bench and smiled—but then flinched at the bruises and stitches on his face and frowned when he admitted being in a bar fight—did you pile on feelings of disgust? No, you let her morph into empathy—even though you knew how she feels about violence.

Review the clips!

Sliptrip, notice that when she couldn't persuade him to come back to the class, her eyes tightened. Exploit that.

Gnatsplat, did you catch your man's annoyance when she pressured him? Awkward! They were both obviously awkward when they met at that bench, but their eyes were alight with interest.

Snuff it out!

Crows in a Tree

Gnatsplat,

You're babbling again. Slow down! So you and Sliptrip failed once more to keep your clients apart—

—it's all Sliptrip's fault! He allowed her to—

—don't interrupt, and don't point fingers! Stick to the facts. So Sliptrip's Miss Prissy took your man to her college class at church and the old anthropology professor who teaches it keeps short-circuiting your strategies.

That's nothing new. That woman is one of the worst of the resilient rebels. Her tempters don't call her Mrs. Gollyglowworm for nothing. So deal with it!

Is that your whole story?

Yes, Devious Master, but you have no idea how this old woman spins us off in all directions. She's on to us! She's like an apostle come to life, talking about "the world, the flesh, and the devil" in ways that rip off the masks. With students hanging around her like crows in a tree, she opens her Bible and says all those things we ridicule all the time, and just as I'm trying to angle my way into my client's thoughts she quotes Carrie Fisher and—

—What are you talking about?

—She's the Star Wars—

—I know who she is, but what's she got to do with it?

She quoted Carrie Fisher saying that sometimes you can only find heaven by slowly backing away from hell.

She went on and on, grabbing more attention by quoting stuff that shouldn't work at all, but it does with these stupid kids, really current, tangly stuff we can't untangle fast enough to get through, and it's all Sliptrip's fault for letting his out-of-control girl force her way back into my boy's life and—

—Stop beating a dead horse! So Sliptrip failed to stop his woman from hauling your man to church. That doesn't get you off the hook.

Yes, Master, true, but this old woman teacher has been urging them to listen for heaven-sent whispers, and even worse, that they have to discern where the whispers are coming from. She even quoted Mother Teresa—

So what?

She said, "Don't believe all the thoughts the devil puts into your head!" That's what she quoted from Mother Teresa—not something about rescuing babies or loving the dying but, "Don't believe all the thoughts the devil puts into your head!"

Stop over-reacting, Sliptrip. Dance into your man's head an image of a cartoon devil whispering silliness in someone's ear.

I will, Master, I will, but this old woman was warning them the spirits are clever and active, and when listening to their whispers, they shouldn't be deceived, and then she quoted Jesus saying when the devil lies, he speaks his native language because he's a liar, and the father of lies. She told these students, "Read everything Jesus was saying about his Father and heaven and hell—"

—block that! Above all, block that. Don't let your boy get into the Scriptures and start reading what Jesus said and did! You know how your boy devoured that Calvin and Hobbes book. Keep his fingers off the Scriptures in any form.

The last thing we want is his burrowing down in a corner of the attic and reading the Gospels.

Temper Flare

Sliptrip,

Repeat what you just sent to me about your woman. She actually lost her temper at her father and told him to butt out?

That's new.

That's very promising!

Yes, Devious Master, yes, just this morning! Her father was insisting she was naïve about Sliptrip's boy—that it was very good to get him to church but he was surely in need of more than spiritual resources—considering his years of troubles, he probably needed therapy and mentoring by someone—but not by her.

Definitely not by her!

She snapped at that. And she actually called him a hypocrite—that all his commitment to inspire boys didn't pass the test when the rubber hit the road.

When she showed her temper, it was marvelous the way he turned harsh. And then her reactions to his demands made things really hot!

The incident devastated him . . . shut him down, and suddenly they both left the room.

Splendid! Splendid!

Maybe now we can break through their soul-mate solidarity. But don't be anxious to grab all the credit. Her father's handler, Zitsit, would surely say it was all his doing.

Now get moving and make up for your past failures. Heat up her resentments at her father's interference.

Yesterday you said she's disappointed that Gnatsplat's young man seems sullen. That's progress. Make her doubt she ever should have gone to bat for the boy.

Above all, keep her away from that old anthropology professor! I've been digging into our files on her, and they're full of warnings. Every contact she has with one of our clients triggers red flags. She's a serious scholar who keeps coming back to the wrong stuff. When she studies belief systems, she finds values in them to integrate into her worldview—and then she runs them through the sieve of the Scriptures.

That makes her impervious to our best interpretations.

Here's what's most dangerous for you: in her international travels, she ferrets out enclaves of rebels infecting our strongholds. She learns from them and inspires them . . . and that's what she's doing in that college class at church.

Do something—anything!

Whisper outrageous lies.

Whatever it takes.

Keep your Miss Prissy away from that old woman.

———

Whispers

Gnatsplat,

Stop panicking! We're fully aware this anthropology pro-fessor spreads rebellions wherever she goes, but your job is to get your boy.

But Devious Master, ever since her fight with her father, Sliptrip's woman is determined to keep dragging him to church and that subversive class, and for the fourth week he's been hearing these talks about faith and hope and absorbing them and—.

—But only once a week! Let me remind you that you have him the rest of the time. Make all that theological stuff fade as you churn up his bitterness at getting kicked out of his mother's basement and forced to live in a crummy attic room.

Remember: emotions rule.

Yes, I know, I know, but this professor dramatizes the stories of Isaiah, Samuel, Elijah, Paul . . . all these old guys who got in-structions and inspiration from the Enemy, and after telling their stories she says, "Never ignore a divine nudge or whisper."

My man is listening to all that!

Well, good. That's your opportunity.

Trundle into his mind what he learned in history classes about divine instructions to burn heretics and start holy wars. Those messages, of course, came from us. Or they started out as divine whispers, but we hell-bent them.

We're damnably good at hell-bending their nudges and directives! We take every divine message and twist and turn and shape—

—yes, but the professor keeps revealing our secrets—how to discern our whispers from theirs.

Deal with it! While all the theological talk swirls vaguely in your Basement Boy's head, tease him with his familiar lusts. Awaken the beast in him. Subvert all the gospel talk as irrelevant to his life. Subvert, subvert, subvert:

>Pleasures into addictions;

>Love into betrayals;

>Religious talk into mockery and revenge.

So far you've done fairly well simmering his pleasures into thinner and thinner gruel. Keep him cooped up in that attic room. Cultivate his cynicism and scrub out any stray bits of gratitude.

You have available plenty of greased skids to slide him into our webs.

>6<

THE MAGICAL WOODS

∧∧∧∧∧∧∧

"Accelerate your girl's sampling the edges
of our slides to the dark side."

∧∧∧∧∧∧∧∧

Father/Daughter Chill

Zitsit,

So finally I hear from you about the girl's father—but only after you can crow about your little triumph of their yelling match. Remember all those other times when your client ignored you and cozied up tighter with the celestials? No reports from you then. But now, when he blows up and says things he regrets, you're quick to tell me all about it.

I've been watching your handling him. You'd better be prepared for rough challenges. This intricate dance between father and daughter could change dramatically.

Use every trick to get your man dancing to our tunes.

First, stifle your eagerness to prompt more blowups between your man and his daughter. Their long habit of forgiving each other for trifles could backfire. Just let the fears and resentments smolder and burn deeper.

Second, leverage the father's resentments toward another male's vying for his only daughter's affections. Plant seeds of fear and disdain for Gnatsplat's Basement Boy.

Third, pour self-pity into him—as Sliptrip is doing to his daughter. Your man is far from over the loss of his wife. Leverage that by intensifying his fears of completely losing his daughter's love and respect.

Suggest he exercise more control over her. That should deepen their estrangement.

Slide to the Dark Side

Sliptrip,

You're right—it's ironic. Your girl prays constantly but perceives no response—just when she keeps hearing about divine whispers! We rarely get to savor such developments. Her tumble from her spiritual mountaintop has been highly satisfying.

Yet the Enemy's silences with such believers too often catch inexperienced fiends like you unaware. Dark nights of the soul too often lead to soul-deepening and, worst of all, prayers we cannot penetrate.

Exploit her anxieties—

—that's just what I've been doing, Master, and as you told me, feeding her fears she'll never find a good man and start a family and—

—Add a sour taste. Convince her that religious fervor gives her nothing. Right now is the time to rub raw her resentments when she feels her father uses religious language to question her judgment.

Accelerate your girl's inching toward the edges of our slides down to the dark side.

I will! I will! She's no longer praying for her speech professor— I've been distracting her from that, and from her schoolwork. So she's nervous about standing in front of the class tomorrow to give her final-exam speech.

A fine opportunity! Leverage it well.

———

Bad Men

Tumbletwit,

Don't come whining to me about your Ms. Sourbelly suddenly having dreams of her happy childhood. What should you do? Figure it's those old sniper prayers of Sliptrip's woman and move on.

Infect her dreams with nightmares about our lecherous professor who dumped her, or dreams of pushing him into fast traffic.

So your professor is nostalgic? Fine! Get her to rhapsodize about her post-divorce years of earned-doctorate intensity when she believed she was discovering ultimate truths. Squelch her girlish memories of her father. Or reimagine them for her again, as you did years ago when you used her hatred for her ex to transfer her anger to her father.

Tumbletwit, media images of abusive men give you stockpiles of ammunition. Have her savor all those stories of bad men. That will nicely bleed off into everything.

Don't you dare lose the chemistry!

Prep her for tomorrow's class by whispering that this will be her chance to get back at Sliptrip's girl. Why should she, a tenured PhD, tolerate disrespect? Conjure up deliciously detailed fantasies of sweet revenge.

Let tomorrow's skirmish begin.

———

Frozen

Sliptrip,

What a difference a day makes! I watched your girl's speech from start to finish. Marvelous! My favorite part was when she realized she had frozen and slowly sank into her seat, eyes on the floor.

Yes, it all worked! It all worked!

At first I was afraid she would stay inspired by all that research she'd done for her speech about fear and courage and Eleanor Roosevelt. She had it totally memorized, but as she got into it, I kept making her aware of her professor's glare, and the young man's empty seat in front of her, and then I flashed her a thought about how stupid she sounded to the classmate beside her.

Just then, in mid-sentence, she glanced again at her teacher—and she froze.

I saw it. In fact, I replayed it. Several times.

This girl has never known public failure. Her disconnect from her father short-circuited her brain. We've ground her grit and gumption right out of her.

The trick now is to make sure she doesn't go groveling to the Enemy. Pile on feelings that she screwed up with him and with her father and they've deserted her, yet somehow it's all her fault. Mix guilt with anger at everybody, including the young man who had raised her hopes.

Keep her feeling estranged and ready to lash out.

Above all, don't let her sink to her knees, begging those celestials to come rescue her.

Male Power

Tumbletwit,

So your professor is deciding how to grade the girl's speech. You know your woman wants to gloat—

—but Master, my professor doesn't know what she wants. She didn't gloat when she saw her student freeze and sit down. I couldn't believe it. She turned her head and looked out the window.

She's still bothered by that strange meeting in her office and that celestial light. And she keeps recalling happy childhood memories, even though I do everything to distract her.

Not everything, obviously.

Kill those reveries. Your professor's hunger for her father's love could blend with longings for what she once had with her husband. That could dribble into empathy for males like Gnatsplat's senseless young man.

We've succeeded in producing a nation of basement boys, and your client has done her bit by urging women to give up on men. So keep lurking in her mind all those images of male abusers.

Oh, she despises them all. I've been feeding that for a long time, following the infernal order to prioritize hostility between the sexes.

Emphasize male power as the primary evil! That's the message.

How handy for us that "power corrupts"—power for males and power for females—against each other. That nicely splits the Enemy's mandated alliance between man and woman.

Intensify her bitterness at our lecherous professor. Every time she notices him on campus, stab her with a flash of remembrance of the moment he shoved her out of his apartment.

———

Nourishing Narcissism

Zitsit,

Don't go bragging to me that father and daughter for the first time didn't say grace together last night. They shouldn't be eating together at all.

I watched the clip. Neither would look at the other as they put food on the table, and both were suitably hostile. But as they sat down, probably from habit your client's hand started to move across the table toward her—

—and, Master, that's just when I flooded his mind with fantasies of Sliptrip's boy offering his daughter drugs. No way was I going to let him touch her hand!

Or say grace together. You were absolutely right to panic at the possibility.

Let me review for you why we work so hard to make everyone think saying grace before meals is the practice of old ladies who impose it on insufferably sweet children.

First, saying grace acknowledges the Enemy is there at the table with them.

Second, it acknowledges that all they have, including their breath and their existence, comes from him.

Third, when they join hands and say grace, they feel gratitude—an appallingly healthy emotion. Gratitude of any sort neutralizes our best chemistry. That's why we worked for years to get people to call "Thanksgiving" anything but that.

"Turkey Day"! That's caught on quite well, thanks to Our Father Below. It puts the emphasis where we can exploit it.

Make saying grace seem ridiculous. They know very well that heavenly spirits do not truck food to their homes. Why should they give thanks for what came from their own hard work?

Remember, in nourishing narcissism, it's always self, self, self . . .

Contagious Moods

Gnatsplat,

How fascinating your young man's perceptions of reality! Even though he flips from movies to games to text messages coming from thousands of miles away, he doubts "heaven-sent whispers" are real.

That's progress. And weeks ago I advised you to fade the old anthropology prof's spiritual talks into background noise. Now you say he barely hears them . . .

Thank you, Master, for all your good advice! I've gotten him into lots of his old habits, and since bad moods are contagious, Sliptrip's woman absorbs his crabbiness. The only reason she's still taking him to these classes is out of duty.

We've doused those sparks in their eyes.

Perfect! Keep your boy in that drafty old attic.

You say he thinks about his mother a lot? Make sure it's proper thinking—dwelling on her betrayal and all the years she kept opening her bed to exploitive men who made her life and his life miserable.

You have plenty of savory ingredients to keep his anger acidic while his subconscious is in turmoil. But keep mother and son apart—you never know what ice might be melted by actual contact.

A Thousand Black Dancers

Sliptrip,

What catastrophic news!

How could this happen, you putrid stink-bomb? Yesterday your woman was spiraling toward us, dispirited and empty, with a dose of rebellious self-righteousness.

You incompetent little fiend! We want a full report of how you were completely outmaneuvered by those conniving spirits.

But Devious Master, I had her all wrapped up in herself all afternoon, but as she was walking by the lake, a flock of starlings erupted from the trees. She kept her eyes on them as they flew away like a thousand black dancers against the sky and they swooped and turned and then dove into the forest, and she kept staring at where they had disappeared. Then she looked up at the white clouds in a dark-blue sky and her tears started, and I have no idea what they were about because as she started walking into the woods I couldn't go with her.

Sliptrip, stop telling a story and make your point. What do you mean you couldn't go with her?

As she approached the forest trail, she began sobbing and crying out to enemy spirits and as she started walking into the woods, something stopped me from going in with her, something cold, like a hard wall of glass.

The last of her thoughts that I caught were about the burr oaks and wildflowers and a bench on the trail.

She was in there for a long, long time, and when she came out from all those trees with their new spring leaves, she was singing with excruciating exuberance those awful praise songs.

I really hate spring—too much symbolism, and too much rebirth and bird song, and it wasn't fair, it definitely wasn't fair—the way they kept me from going with her. They have too many advantages!

Buck up, miserable fiend! When you're at war, you get shot at and sabotaged. That doesn't excuse your bewilderment—which I've critiqued before.

Master, with all due respect, I don't think I'm bewildered but trying every minute to get through to her, but the singing and praising and praying and her syrupy thoughts about her father make it like fighting through a grenade field.

I simply can't connect with her.

If you can't, another fiend will. No mortal is impervious.

PART THREE

INTERMISSION

Once more, take a break from these diabolical messages.

As you might imagine, while we worked on this project our staff had spirited discussions about evil forces in our world versus forces of light and beauty and joy. Names of evil dictators who caused horrific miseries for millions were contrasted with names of selfless and joyous saints who brought hope to the world. What, we asked, was really at the heart of our world's troubles?

It's not surprising that for millennia men and women have wondered the same things and have been writing about evil spirits active in human affairs. Here are additional selected quotations to ponder:

<><><>

My subject in fiction is the action of grace in territory largely held by the devil.

—Flannery O'Connor

<><><>

One day the angels came to present themselves before the Lord, and Satan also came with them. The Lord said to Satan, "Where have you come from?" Satan answered the Lord, "From roaming throughout the earth, going back and forth in it."

—Job 1

<><><>

From his brimstone bed at break of day, a walking
the devil is gone,
To visit his snug little farm the earth, and see how
his stock goes on.
—Samuel Taylor Coleridge

<><><>

The devil keeps man from good with a thousand machinations
. . . he teaches him that he can set his own law for himself.
—Hildegard of Bingen

<><><>

The devil is a better theologian than any of us and is a devil still.
—A. W. Tozer

<><><>

The devil said to Jesus, "If you are the Son of God, tell these
stones to become loaves of bread." But Jesus told him, "No! The
Scriptures say, 'People do not live by bread alone, but by every
word that comes from the mouth of God.'"
—Matthew 4

<><><>

The reason the Son of God appeared was to destroy
the devil's work.
—1 John 3

<><><>

To admire Satan is to give one's vote not only for a world of
misery, but also for a world of lies.
—C. S. Lewis

<><><>

Jesus' disciples joyfully reported to him, "Lord, even the demons
obey us when we use your name." He told them, "Yes, I saw
Satan fall from heaven like lightning! Look, I have given you
authority over all the power of the enemy . . ."
—Luke 10

<><><>

Be alert. Your enemy the devil prowls around like a roaring lion
looking for someone to devour.
—1 Peter 5

<><><>

Satan prowls, but he's a lion on a leash.
—Ann Voskamp

<><><>

>7<

CELESTIAL CHICANERY

∧∧∧∧∧∧

"Few things are as repugnant to us as father/daughter magic."

∧∧∧∧∧∧∧∧

—

Wild Card

Slinkbog,

Think long and hard about Sliptrip's fate. Shudder as you envision the consequences of his incompetence in allowing his woman's spiritual resurgence.

As his successor, don't suppose your greater experience makes you immune from his failures. His woman—now yours—has alarmed all of us. Your Miss Prissy is capable of spreading that light she's dancing in, and you're charged to drag her out of it.

Devious Master, with the greatest respect, I acknowledge my great responsibility and assure you I will night and day stay zeroed in on my client with all my expertise. My track record speaks for itself and—

—your track record doesn't include seducing souls as vitalized as this woman. I can't emphasize enough that after her dark night of the soul and the conflagration in the woods, she's a wild card.

She'll challenge you in ways you won't expect.

Yes, Master, I have been studying her history and—

—Remember this—you are just as replaceable as Sliptrip. They didn't name us Legion for nothing—you imps are everywhere, like hordes of insects, and in an instant you can be squashed like one and scraped off into your true home.

But for now, you have the chance to prove your mettle.

Already she's reconciled with her father. How disgusting it was to watch them forgiving each other with those pernicious tears and hugs and mawkish laughter—the exact opposite of our bitter laughter and tears of despair.

Few things are as repugnant to us as father/daughter magic.

Use every wedge, every possible resentment, every misunderstanding, to deaden their dad/daughter music. Tell her as she prays blessings on her father and all those others that her prayers are useless.

You can spin almost any event as evidence prayer is simply talking to one's self.

This woman knows better than that, of course. But as her sense of the Enemy's presence comes and goes, keep telling her it's capricious and not real. Hit her with doubts at strategic moments.

Fortunately, she's seeing no results of her prayers for Gnatsplat's Basement Boy since she has no idea where he is.

Keep it that way.

<hr />

Bar Talk

Gnatsplat,

Your barely concealed glee about Sliptrip's removal from Miss Prissy's care will turn to terror if you think you can glide along and enjoy the show. Your boy is nicely stuck in our sticky strands, but that woman's prayers put you on high alert.

You never know what chicanery those celestials may be up to.

Let's review the best cards in your deck:

>His hatred of his mother burns a bit hotter each day.

>We've convinced him church talk is made-up noise.

>He's self-medicating his woes in bars, where interesting things happen . . .

Your client is edging toward desperation, and desperate men do desperate things. That opens up all sorts of options. Get him some new rough-and-tumble friends. As he commiserates in those bars, have him transfer some of his inner rage to the men around him.

Let the liquor flow. Loosen his tongue.

———

Male Breakdown

Gnatsplat,

Your last message was incoherent. Stop blasting words at me! Start over and slow down. What happened?

It was that damn box!

What box?

A cigar box. My guy went into his mother's house looking for his sweater. She's a hoarder, and he started moving her piles of stuff. Shoving and lifting, he noticed his name on a little box halfway under a blanket. When he picked it up his mother yelled, "That's mine!" and grabbed for it, but he held it out of reach and saw his birth date under his name. She clawed at him, trying to get the box, screaming, "Give it to me, give it to me, give it to me!" but he pulled away and ducked out of the house.

Inside the box he found photos and notes and poems from when he was a baby and he read and reread the notes and poems and stared forever at the pictures—

—So get to the point.

The point is what happened when that woman tracked him down.

What woman?

Sliptrip's woman, of course! Er . . . Slinkbog's! She's a pest and a fly in the eye.

My boy was sitting on a bench in an old playground near his mother's house. I'd been whispering to him for hours, but he'd gotten emotional about his mother, thinking she still loved him since she cared so much about the box. He was reading her notes and inspiring poems about loving children—

I hate those treacly poems! I hate the way women are with their babies.

Everything in that box was treacly! He was remembering his mother when she loved him, and he was softening up, listening to other whispers—but I kept telling him his mother was selfish, she wanted the box only for herself and she had proven she didn't love him because what mother would never, ever stand up for her son—and I had him!

But then she came. Slinkbog's woman!

Somehow she had tracked him down, and at first she just sat beside him. His face was hard, staring at the old playground equipment halfway sunk into the grass. But I could tell she was breathing with those celestials. She was praying for my client. She reached over and touched him.

Instantly, I was slammed away from them.

Those intrusive, scheming spirits! They're cheating, and that infuriating, prissy woman has become full of their celestial energies!

She's like a Joan of Arc come alive!

You know nothing at all about Joan of Arc.

But this woman is like what I've heard about her, all purpose and horrific holiness! All I could do was shudder as she looked into that box with him and—

If you keep whining about your failures, you'll have lots more to shudder about.

<hr/>

The Mother's Cigar Box

So, Slinkbog . . .

. . . you bragged that your years of experience would equip you to handle this woman. Now your Miss Prissy is not only endangering our grip on Gnatsplat's boy but she's putting his mother's soul at risk.

What's the matter with you? At least when Sliptrip was handling her she didn't—

—But, Devious Master, when I was charged with her seduction, she was already in an abysmally beatific state! I'm blocked out from her because she keeps praying and praising and confessing, and she smiles all the time at what those celestials slip into her thoughts.

Even before she reached out on that bench and touched Gnatsplat's boy, I used every tactic to stop her. But she kept gently drawing him out, using those cigar-box memories and that smile of hers. She listened to all his troubles, and every time she smiled at him, you could see his hopes rising. That's when romantic sparks started flashing.

They were like fireflies in the dark, and I could do nothing, <u>*nothing.*</u>

Then she offered to take the box back to the mother! Everywhere our alarms were blaring. I was horribly aware she was a threat to all of us.

—You were aware, but so what? You were with her, and it was on you to reset the—

—*Yes, Master, yes, but all of us were blocked from getting through. And when she took that memory box to his mother, knocking on her door and then smooth-talking her way in, it didn't matter that we all crowded in with her, poking our elbows at the Enemy's rebel spirits who were coming in with her.*

Somehow she got the boy's mother all teary/bleary-eyed over those photos and notes. Not once did my girl wince at the stinky couch she was sitting on.

After she left, the whole house felt like Enemy territory.

Master, I assure you all of us—

—and I assure you, Slinkbog, we saw you and the other deplorable misfits cringing in all that light and scurrying around stupidly like beheaded chickens.

Get your eyes off the ground!

We will not tolerate these invasions of our territories.

At Last a Smackdown!

Tumbletwit,

Finally, after all your wobbling around, and after all your failures, you tightened your grip on your client!

You've had a lot of help. The rumors on campus that mad-as-hell students would soon expose our lecherous professor filled your professor with triumphal expectations. She now envisions his paying big time for his crime, and she relishes every new rumor.

That set her up to finally put little Miss Prissy in her place.

We loved watching her come into your professor's office all bright-eyed and bushy-tailed, thinking since she'd gotten through to the boy and his mother, she could work her magic there. Hah! She had no idea how much you'd heated up your client's wrath at being disrespected.

What a satisfying moment! The girl entered all sweetness and purpose—but defenseless against your professor's jarring volley of attacks. She was smacked down like a bird hitting a window. Whack!

Little Miss Prissy had no idea of how to counter your professor's brilliant deconstructions of her beliefs. The girl has been neutralized . . . for the moment.

Tumbletwit, keep energizing your professor with this new sense of power from knowing her ex-lover will soon be exposed. Every time she sees him on campus, have her smile about his coming take-down.

And very important right now—deepen her intellectual silo. The more intense her certainties, the more opportunities for you . . .

Savory Verbiage

Slinkbog,

You got quite a break when your feisty Miss Prissy was stunned by Tumbletwit's professor. She's fallen from what you called her Joan of Arc moment, so stop complaining about the celestials still hovering over her.

Splinter her spiritual momentum. Start with her father by making her wonder what he's really thinking. He's worried our Basement Boy will seduce his daughter and drag her down. He can't hide the fact he hates her spending so much time with him.

Keep whispering to her that her dad's a hypocrite, and that he doesn't really trust her.

We hear Gnatsplat has been shipping boatloads of savory verbiage your way. He's throwing tantrums over the fact your woman has gotten his boy a place to stay with old Mrs. Gollyglowworm.

That could mean big trouble for Gnatsplat . . . but not necessarily for you.

The anthropology professor takes in all sorts of strays—male and female—but she can't change our Basement Boy overnight. Your Miss Prissy will think, since he has a place to stay, a mentor, and a job at Starbucks, he'll follow through on all his promises.

Hah! We know Gnatsplat will see that he doesn't.

When your woman hears he still goes into bars at night, she'll feel betrayed. Fuel those feelings. Keep her self-absorbed. As always, her emotional peaks and valleys are your openings.

On a peak, let her look down on others as inferior. When low, flood her with doubts.

Frequently urge her to ask why the Enemy took away her beloved mother. Slip in a tang of bitterness.

The Un-Welcome Home

Gnatsplat,

Sometimes events turn out advantageous for us when we had nothing to do with setting them up. It was Slinkbog's prissy woman who came up with the idea that she and your Basement Boy should visit his mother together.

How naïve!

She thought she had it figured out. Knowing how emotional his mother was about her memory box and his childhood, and knowing your boy's longings, she persuaded him to go. She figured she'd help them reconcile . . . that the mother's gratitude for the groceries she had been bringing her and their surface chatter meant she'd made a friend.

She had—but a friend we'd long ago hollowed out.

The minute the mother opened the door to them, her man in the next room was out of his chair. When he saw her son with a young woman, he set his teeth and his fists.

That, Gnatsplat, was the payoff moment for all these days you've kept your boy smoldering about the man who kicked him out of his house. When the older man threatened him, his fury burst.

Yes, yes, it was marvelous. My boy ferociously hammered the guy with his fists, and his mother just stood there while his girlfriend stifled a scream. He bolted out the door, with his mother yelling at him.

Perfect. Now dig into your toolbox of guilt and estrangement and mix that with oily satisfaction at nailing the guy.

Keep revenge scenarios popping up in his head.

Bawdy Poem Seductions

Tumbletwit,

I'm sure you've heard our randy professor has now been exposed everywhere in the national press—

—Yes! Yes! For years my woman would seethe at rumors about his seducing students, but now she's ear-to-ear smiles as she pores over all the reports. She's called two of the former students accusing him to cheer them on.

Marvelous! While at one end of campus you've been basting your Ms. Sourbelly in our juices for years, on the other end we've been whispering to our tenured prof that seducing girls is simply what males do. He wove his slick skills with bawdy-poem discussions with hints the girls' grades depended on their understanding the poems' meanings . . . in his apartment, of course.

Now, as his victims are getting their revenge—

—Yes, my client is helping them . . . and yesterday, as her ex-lover sat in the faculty lounge with his hunted look and his expansive belly, she stared at him accusingly, with disgust and contempt.

—And her hatred will get even hotter when she hears him insist he was "just doing what's natural" and that everything these women are describing was consensual.

We'll savor his growing terror, and strategically we'll hype his blustering and counterattacking. That will fuel the rage that will ricochet into every corner of the campus, and certainly the office of your Ms. Sourbelly.

It will! It will! It's already ricocheting, with rumors flying about other guilty professors and staff. They're hiding in the woodwork, terrified they'll be dragged in.

All the accusations and the hatreds for the man my professor hates makes her feel vindicated and powerful—and wide open to my suggestions.

Hitch a ride with her! And don't forget another sweet spot: incite her to spread her hatred to women who stand up for men caught in the crossfire. Lure your professor into launching a withering attack on those women.

That could provide all sorts of dynamics for us. Stoke those fires white-hot.

———

A Timely Crash

Gnatsplat,

Amazing what liquor can do! Two young men in the middle of the night in the same old bar telling the same old stories are suddenly walking out the door intent on beating each other in a race on their battered old motorcycles . . .Basement Boy and buddy well liquored up . . . how promising is that?

Ah, alcohol—our all-purpose, ubiquitous tool! What would we do without it?

I'm sure you're taking credit for getting your man to accept the challenge in the bar. You're surely congratulating yourself for revving him up to accelerate on the curve so he'd spin off into the trees. But as he now lies in the dark with broken ribs under the weight of the machine, don't get distracted. Don't simply enjoy his horror at realizing he is dying alone in the night.

As you know so well, the dying often cry out for mercy.

Don't let that happen.

Keep his mind busy. Fan the embers of anger that his inebriated friend roared off in triumph, oblivious. Have him ask over and over, *Where's my buddy? Why isn't he coming back?*

Keep blowing on those embers, and use the pain and fear to blame somebody, anybody.

He's alone in the dark woods.

Hover over him.

Steer every thought.

Ease him into our welcoming hands.

Night Alert

No, Slinkbog,

. . . your panicked, middle-of-the-night message did not disorient me. You say your anthropologist is sitting up in bed wide awake praying?

Not good! These disruptive spirits take every opportunity to catch imps like you off guard. And you say she's praying for Gnatsplat's boy?

Whoa!

Stop those prayers *now, now, now!*

Quick! Get her thinking she's reacting to a bad dream or something she ate. Don't let this woman of yours change everything by praying at the worst possible moment.

The boy she's been trying to save is dying in the woods. Stifle those prayers!

But how could she know about the boy?

She doesn't. She knows nothing, but her suddenly praying for him in the night, upright in bed, proves those celestials are maddeningly active right now. They're trying to cheat us of our rightful prey.

Blunt their interference.

Distort their whispers.

Make her thoughts a tangle of confusions, with doses of bewilderment at being awakened deep in the night.

Prayers change things.

They're virile and dangerous.

Get her head back on her pillow.

———

Conniving Celestials

Gnatsplat,

One moment you're in a crash scene watching your prey in the woods breathe ever closer to our grasping hands, and the next you're in over your head.

What a difference a few minutes make!

For once I can't blame your incompetence. Those celestial spirits crossed the line when they awakened Slinkbog's woman to pray!

Right now they're active all over your territory.

And, Gnatsplat, don't ask me how those spirits had the gall to get that old anthropology prof involved! Yes, that searchlight you see coming toward you is held by her thin and wrinkled hand. Can't you see her swinging it as she's calling out for your boy?

Those conniving spirits' alerting her is *outrageous* interference! They've become so involved with this woman that they've practically made her one of them. She knows much too much! Somehow she ended up right where she shouldn't be. The old meddler should be home asleep moaning about old-age pains, not stumbling in the dark through the woods trying to rescue a drunk.

Do anything and everything to stop your boy from seeing or hearing her.

Keep his eyes on the blood from his chest soaking into his shirt.

Make him wince at the sharp pains of his broken ribs so he won't see the light she's carrying.

At all costs, stop that interfering old woman from reaching your man.

>8<

HANDCUFF GLEE

^^^^^^

*"Rage is flying like bits of hot shrapnel,
ever since our pervy poet did his perp walk."*

^^^^^^^

Teetering on a Tall Pole

Gnatsplat,

You haven't yet met Sliptrip's fate, but you're close. Very close. What a debacle you allowed!

When your man was crumpled under his motorcycle, you failed to stop his fingers on his cell from getting off a text to that interfering old woman. And when she got there with her searchlight swinging and kept calling out to him, your brain must have melted. You kept watching those flashes from her light that ignited all that hope in his eyes.

But I messaged you and asked what to do and—

Don't blame me, you senseless, slimy slug! You panicked and did nothing. That old meddler kept calling out to him, moving with all those celestials in the woods, and you were a glassy-eyed rodent in the weeds.

Think about our Basement Boy's transformation as he saw the old woman approaching. You can be assured you will always, always regret what happened to him in that moment.

Gnatsplat, it is only by your good fortune we have no one less addled to replace you. At the moment, that is . . .

Get hold of yourself and reclaim your man! Fail, and you know what's in store. We will not accept his rising from death's brink into the arms of the Enemy.

Lure him back!

I will, I will, Devious Master, and I am already making him question why—

Don't mess with logic—go for his gut. Make him feel furious he ended up under the motorcycle and the other guy kept going. His new alliance with the Enemy doesn't make him immune to the hooks we've embedded in him.

Right now he feels everything's changed and that he's a new person. But as his relief at being alive begins to ebb, you'll find him teetering on a slender pole of his history and habits.

Day after day, use those hooks . . . use them all to convince him his true identity is with us.

Peter the Wimp

Slinkbog,

Wake up, sluggard!

It's clear to us you're failing to blunt your woman's fervent prayers. Her suddenly sitting up in bed praying right after the motorcycle crash ruined our great chance with Gnatsplat's boy. Never, ever take prayers lightly!

Don't you remember all our warnings about this odious activity they call intercession? Prime example: Peter with his impetuous personality was our easy target—we used fear, shame, and dread to seduce him into denying Jesus. But of all the calamities that could happen to us in this battlefield, it was *Jesus himself* who prayed for him—"interceded" for him.

So what happened to Peter the weak-willed wimp? He became a rock, fearless, unashamed, spreading trouble for us everywhere he went.

You've got to jam these communications. She's praying for far too many of our prey—the professor, the boy's mother . . . even the mother's boyfriend.

Your woman's father is just as bad. Zitsit can barely get a bit of bitterness lodged into him about his wife's death. The man is always praying.

Here's the worst part of their praying for others: the Spirit of the Enemy joins them and empowers them. That has withering impact on our most heroic efforts.

Block these noxious prayers. And while you're at it, stop your woman from taking groceries to the boy's mother. No good will come of that.

Gleeful View of Handcuffs

Tumbletwit,

How sweet the sounds of outraged accusations.

How doubly sweet the panicked denials! So many openings for us . . . so many souls in play . . . so much to savor . . .

Yes, yes, yes, rage is flying like bits of hot shrapnel everywhere on campus, ever since our pervy poet did his perp walk. My exuberant PhD canceled her class so they all could see him led away in handcuffs, and then she watched the news clip over and over again . . . and when they let him out on bail, she rallied students to protest—

—We saw that, and when she got home she plopped herself on the couch and watched the handcuffs clip again and again.

It's been most entertaining! Yet your Ms. Sourbelly knows what happens to women who speak out, so she's not about to tell her own story . . . which gives you interesting leverage . . .

Your woman is jubilant in a frothy mix of guilt and confusion—

—Oh, she's all lit up for us, transfixed by the stories she's hearing and triumphant that he's like a worm on a hook. Yet she's also scared by the media coverage and worries she might say something that will snap back at her.
She's already been targeted by trolls.

How advantageous! As she hears more stories from the accusers and sees our man's denials, your job is to keep her vindictive.

We have fascinating scenarios forming just now. She just may be bitter enough to make something really interesting happen.

———

Infectious Testimony

Gnatsplat,

We are getting a raft of complaints from your fellow fumblers about the way you let your young man share his story in front of the whole church. They're especially incensed about all those college students hearing it. They say it's alerting far too many to what we're doing.

Who can blame these tempters for complaining? A previously tongue-tied basement boy tells of his barroom challenge and his roaring heedless into a turn on the road and crashes. From the pit of near-death in the night woods, he sees a lantern's light. An old woman gets him out from under the crumpled wheel and—as he put it—"into light from above."

No wonder our demons cringed! The boy's story and faith are infectious. Our priorities for church talks are to foster pride, hypocrisy, tribalism, boredom . . . never stories about light and redemption.

Your only hope, Gnatsplat, is to reverse the drama. Seduce him into a whole new story.

All the young women in the church now view him differently. There's your opening. Use your creativity and his jaded experiences to drag him into his old ways.

Our recent successes in this culture should make that easy.

Once you get him into bed with one or more of these church girls, you have more than enough to work with. Jealousies, gossip, meanness . . . have him do things to provoke the girls to turn on him and to start stories buzzing around the church that will make his drama of a night-time conversion seem like pure poppycock.

Cracking Resistance

Zitsit,

Don't you dare blow the opportunities in front of you.

So Gnatsplat's man is now in our Enemy's camp and his dramatic story is making the church vermin squirm around in bliss? You and I know those white clouds of joy in them and in the girl's father are full of gray streaks for you to darken.

Keep the father/daughter tensions simmering. Have him warn her over and over that the boy is not suddenly an angel but still a male with a history. Every time she brushes her father off, heighten his need to control her.

At the same time, don't think heating up conflicts is the end game. Keep the main thing the main thing—seducing his soul.

Here's a way to make him one of ours: Bubbling in his subconscious is his hidden wish the boy was still in his old ways. When he catches himself realizing he'd accept almost anything to keep his daughter bonded to him instead of this kid, seed in guilt.

In addition, add anger at his daughter for not caring enough that he's lost his wife and desperately needs his girl's loyalty. Drill down on getting him absorbed in self.

Remember our mantra: self, self, self is the slick slide to our webs.

Hot Chili Peppers

Slinkbog and Gnatsplat,

So, my dynamic duo, can you feel our hot breath on your necks? We've charged you both with tempting these two rebel agents raising holy heaven against us. What in hell's name are you doing to break them up?

Nothing that we can see! You indolent imps are too busy shouting insults and blame at each other—puking into foul winds that gust it all back on both of you. So there you are, puke on your faces, watching them working together at the church food pantry.

Each time they do some goody-goody project together, they cuddle up closer. Can't you see they're like a scene from a Hallmark movie? Sickening!

Gnatsplat, your boy is fascinated by her insisting on sexual boundaries, and his intrigue about that makes her more and more desirable to him. Wait for just the right moment when they're alone and they kiss. Goad him inch by inch to take her much further than she'll allow.

Whisper to him that she really wants it . . . despite her resistance.

Slinkbog, your part is to muddle her mind so she assumes his new spiritual intensity means he'll act honorably in all the ways important to her. Use her state of falling in love with him—and her desires when she's in his arms—to keep her naïve.

Naïve enough that she'll be drawn like a moth to a flame . . .

And Gnatsplat, your job is to make him a flame! If he forces her, she'll believe he's like all these other men she's reading about, and this little Hallmark movie comes to a satisfying end.

Travel Temptations

Gnatsplat,

You and Slinkbog must be ignoring my flood of suggestions. How hard is it to sabotage a romance?

Your boy's spiritual intensity keeps lifting Miss Prissy's respect for him, and he can't believe she's actually falling in love with him. Her loyalty and delight in him keeps amazing your Basement Boy, and it's making him into a new person.

At all costs, shut this down.

Get them squabbling, or lying in bed together full of guilt and anger. Take any strategy I've sent you—any one of them—and make it happen!

The only promising thing right now is that they'll be apart for a few weeks. Don't blow your opportunities when he's on the mission trip he signed up for and she's at home taking exams. Your boy will be traveling with mostly young women and old retirees—a perfect mix. He's bound to say things to offend the retirees, and the young women—well, obviously, get him involved with one.

Make him do something so he'll look dirty, guilty, and a terrible choice to bring on a mission trip.

Dad/Daughter Rift

Slinkbog,

Perfect timing!

At last you brought the simmering parent/child discord to a boil and tipped it over the edge. Your woman's angrily moving out of her father's house opens a whole new playing field.

Get her obsessed with her father's parting shot about her lack of appreciation as she walked out. Link her plummeting emotions to his warnings about the boy.

Stir up new conflicts.

Heighten her anxieties about her moving in with a self-absorbed friend of hers. Whisper doubts about her decision to skip the mission trip. Repeat over and over about the young man: *What is he really doing down there?*

Create some naughty scenarios.

Your woman has always lived with highs and lows. Now you can leverage them. This break with her father, and her anxiety about the young man she fears hasn't really changed, may make her finally vulnerable.

Remind her of how much she prays for that never changes. Remember these two things from your training:

>When a client feels empty and unmotivated yet keeps on praying, those prayers are the most dangerous. Distract her! Don't let her pray like that.

>Prayers are as strong a force as gravity. Watch out for what they might unleash.

Starbucks and the World

Gnatsplat,

How tiresome you are! The reports on your failures are like flea bites—irritating . . . making us long to crush some small, loathsome insect.

Like you, irksome imp.

What are you doing down there on that mission trip—luxuriating in the sunshine? You're in one of our strongholds on this planet, so why no results? We're told your guy is up to his armpits in mud, loving destitute kids swarming around him, and even worse, he's feeling empathy for their mother who has nothing but eight hungry ragamuffins and rusty sheets of metal for a roof.

Don't you realize this is the worst possible outcome? He's starting to revel in having a purpose—to help and protect these people. That can undo years of our chipping away at his masculine identity.

This trip is when you're supposed to draw him back into his old habits . . . into violating taboos so the old geezers in the group will judge him. But you're letting him remember those Starbucks books and how they apply to his helping these people. He's reading this stuff on his phone and relating it to the Scriptures on all those sites with multiple translations.

Stop all that! Your boy is going at it the way he used to play video games.

Worst of all, he's promised the mother of these ragamuffins he'll come back and build her some kind of shelter. How did you let those celestials get their way with your guy? All this fire in his belly and all those plans dancing in his head are pointing him up, not down.

Get to him.

Cripple all that before he boards the plane home.

Something Snapped

Tumbletwit,

What amusing creatures these humans are! Your esteemed professor, for all her years of academic discipline, is now becoming an addled specimen.

How disorienting for her that our perv's defense attorney is a woman. Your client was infuriated when she saw our self-assured attorney using legal tricks to free our randy poetry scholar. Our female lawyer accused his female accusers, staring dismissively into the cameras. Your professor hated that!

But then came the best of all. When our obviously guilty professor claimed to reporters that all was consensual—gloating he'd beat the "outrageous charges"—something in your Ms. Sourbelly snapped.

Yes, Master, and so suddenly and strangely . . . now she keeps aimlessly pacing her office and lecturing herself to do the smart thing—yet she hates the fact that no matter how she tries to concentrate, she can't figure out what the smart thing is.

I keep reminding her of how horrific it is that the monster she thought had finally been exposed and nailed is instead getting away with sexual harassment and rape.

She frowns into a mirror.

She smears at it with her palm.

She snarls at her reflection . . .

I think of her as our lab animal trapped in our maze of mirrors. It's fascinating how she keeps looking everywhere online, clicking from site to site, searching for ammunition against our guy, but when she finds rough stuff, she doesn't know what to do with it.

Yes! Yes! She lands on all sorts but then just moves on, and she's listening to me again, really listening, and she's using lots more of those prescription drugs she's been trying to shake . . .

Her belly may be churning and her brain incoherent, but one thing she's clear on . . . she hates our perv professor with all the intensity you've helped burn into her.

>9<

SALVATION ARMY BLUES

∧∧∧∧∧∧

"That book revived her treacherous Joan of Arc intensity."

∧∧∧∧∧∧∧

Stoking Rebellious Desires

Slinkbog,

Since your woman moved out of her father's house, you've done a few things right. There was that moment when her pastor quoted Jesus saying, "My Father's house will be your house," and she got all teary, thinking about good times in her dad's house. You nicely sidetracked her from warm thoughts and back into their last argument when she felt kicked out and orphaned.

Yet that counts for little. After moving out, your woman was confused and vulnerable, a lost calf in lion country—and you should have pounced. Her spat with her father plus second thoughts about the young man and all that time staring stone-faced at the wall as her prayers bounced off it . . . she was easy pickings.

But you let her pick up the wrong book.

Terrible move! Her reading about the early lives of William and Catherine Booth and their founding the Salvation Army changed everything.

How, you mush-brained imbecile, could you have let her touch that book? Reading about the desperately poor and sick in London made her think of poor and desperate families she serves at her church. Reading about William and Catherine's compulsion to actually do something—to bring hope and practical help—made her think of the young man on the mission trip doing just that.

The Salvation Army!

Of all the pernicious tales she should *not* be reading, what could be worse than the story of a man and a woman together doing the work of the Enemy in extreme circumstances? The book crisped up her determination to pray through her spiritual dryness. She's praying for her father and for Sliptrip's man and his mother. And you need to know we're alarmed she's once again praying through her visceral dislike for our Ms. Sourbelly.

She's praying for her soul!

You know what we think about intercessory prayer.

Her reading and rereading that book revived her treacherous intensity, stoking her desires for a spiritual, heroic partnership. Unfortunately the young man will soon return, and Gnatsplat has utterly failed to seduce his client.

Slinkbog, think of all the troubles we've had from the Salvation Army for more than a century! These two, if they get together, could do us horrific damage.

Commitment Hell

Gnatsplat,

The desperation in your messages draws no sympathy from me. What did you expect would happen when your man got back from his trip on which you were supposed to trip him up and expose him as a fraud? He's become like a little wind in the tropics, sucking up heat and moisture and blowing stronger and stronger, threatening to become a hurricane.

Yes, your client is still full of the baggage we got into him, but your allowing all those camaraderie moments in that village around campfires singing those sickeningly sweet choruses that mock us . . . face it—you've created a monster.

Your boy's awakenings among those indigenous believers who see us but defy us was wretched . . . and that horrific welcome back at the airport was even worse. Bad enough Miss Prissy was in the crowd—but her father, too, with a big grin and his arms wide for the boy.

That poured more fuel on his rebellious spirit, and it started healing what we've been rubbing raw for years.

A *father* was loving him. Very bad news for us.

Zitsit was told to keep her father out of that airport, but he failed miserably. He escorted boy and daughter to his car, drove them to a restaurant, celebrated in a cozy booth all the stories your client told about the trip. Now they're all three part of the rebellious community empowering each other against us.

You're so right, Devious Master, because Zitsit wrecked our chances to get hold of my boy again, and Slinkbog lets his Miss Prissy dance her way past him day after day as she consorts with those obsequious spirits who keep telling her to obey like they do. So she just fires up, and she and my boy have been laughing together again at Calvin and Hobbes "like old times," and she teases him but in ways that do us no good at all and just make him laugh and—

—Stop!

Get real, Gnatsplat. Shifting the blame helps you not a bit. Your job is to get through to your liberated Spiderboy. Convince him that all this romancing is deadly pixie dust. It's luring him into the rusty manacles of marriage.

Miss Prissy keeps blinking in amazement at your boy's transformation, believing her wish has come true that he'll be her William Booth. She wants marriage. Yesterday when they kissed both their heads were full of hopes and promises.

Derail this train!

Here's how:

Find a way to get him revisiting those websites warning men that marriage is slavery. Remind him that women initiate divorce far more than men do and that—once divorced—he'd be stuck with child support, with none of the benefits.

Drill into him what he's seen on those sites: "After the wedding, your life is over."

Plug his ears against church talk promoting the joys of rising to responsibilities and caring for others. The last thing we want is men protecting and nurturing their children—especially rebels who have joined Enemy forces.

Flashbacks and Reactions

Tumbletwit,

So your Ms. Sourbelly is not only flipped out but she's nourishing your seeds of deadly intent.

Terrific!

But stop preening like a berserk peacock. Once again you're trying to grab credit for years of work by your betters. All those rape stories your client has been listening to with her emotions spinning like loose flywheels—where do you think those crimes came from?

You're the beneficiary of years of masterful cultivation of males by a long line of tempters.

—Yes, Master, I understand, and I'm continuing to instigate my professor's night flashbacks and maximizing her stunned reaction to the judge's disallowing half the women's testimonies.

—Keep boiling those pots.

Your Sourbelly's mix of fury and tipsiness as she ups her prescription dosages means you may soon discover rare opportunities.

The Wooden Peasant

Gnatsplat,

So your boy is still carrying around that little carving he got on his mission trip. You were told right away to get rid of it! What's your problem?

I keep trying to get his attention but he holds it tight in his hand, or he feels its rough edges with his fingertips, or he puts it carefully into that fancy box he found, or—

—That's the point—he's too involved with it. You need to find a way to get it lost, and here's why:

First, when the old guy down there who carved it gave it to him, the first thing your boy thought of was to give it to Miss Prissy. Stifle that. *Nothing* should further their relationship.

Second, you don't want him carrying around a carving of a peasant in torn clothes with hands clasped high in prayer. It says *all* the wrong things.

Third, it makes him think of that poor old guy who carved it handing it to him with a smile and waving away his offer of payment . . . the same old guy who had been painting church walls with him and humming those insurrectionist spirituals—

—I know, I know, and I've been interrupting those sounds whenever he—

Shut up and listen up!

Fourth, if he does wrap that thing and give it to the girl as a memento of his trip, he'll start telling her his stories all over again—about how the people down there have nothing, but their contentment and hospitality was "so refreshing."

No! Whenever she'd look at that little wooden guy or—hell forbid—carry it in her purse, she'd be thinking of him.

We told you when he was down there to have him fumble with it so when he crossed the rope bridge it would fall into the river, or to have him somehow misplace it in the baggage.

Gnatsplat, get it lost!

Opening Flood Gates

Slinkbog,

Don't you remember what we told you happened when your Miss Prissy suddenly sat up in bed and started praying? It opened the flood gates for those interfering celestials!

You need to shut down her prayers for our Ms. Sourbelly.

Keep reminding your woman of her professor's sarcasm and all-around unpleasantness in her classroom. Let your girl pray about the heathen in far-off lands, not about Tumbletwit's client.

We do not want intrusions right now into our distraught professor's promising trajectory.

The Un-botched Proposal

Gnatsplat and Slinkbog,

A fine pair of idiot imps you two are!

Gnatsplat, for weeks we've been telling you to ditch that wooden peasant he keeps carrying around and to drag him into his old habits. Instead you dithered and now we have this catastrophic proposal.

Both of you had all sorts of chances to disrupt it. Why didn't you take clues from YouTube videos of proposals gone bad, like the woman in front of 10,000 fans walking away from the guy on his knees, or the girl slapping the kneeling young man? Of all the variations of botched proposals, couldn't you engineer just one?

Your passive snoozing—

—But Master I wasn't at all snoozing . . . Gnatsplat should have warned me about his intentions with that carving because it took me by surprise, and—

Snoozing or stupid, it doesn't matter—you both did nothing that worked. Now they're committed to each other.

View the clip again. She's sitting in that ice cream shop opposite him, her fingers wrapped around her frosted glass, when he pulls the carving from his pocket and stands it on the table in front of her . . . a little guy the size of his hand, torn pants, wide-brimmed hat . . . Think of the things you could have whispered at that moment.

When he explained to her the old man had carved it from a chunk of driftwood, and when he described the carver's refusing payment, you should have distracted them with thoughts of money or old age—or *anything*.

Think about it! When he was tracing the peasant's face and praying hands and told her the man was like him, poor and raggedy but with hope in his uplifted face—such smarmy goo bringing tears to her eyes—

—Yes! That's when I whispered to him—

—he never heard you! And, Slinkbog, the instant she saw the ring in his hand—

—But I was caught off guard! Suddenly the ring was between his fingers and he was on his knees asking her to marry him and slipping the ring on her finger and Gnatsplat should have made him fumble the ring or—

—Both of you had hundreds of ways to botch this proposal!

But, Devious Master, you told me to get my girl's pride pumped way up, that I should get her feeling a stronger sense of entitlement because, as you explained, if I spun her "high and holy purpose" into—

—Don't don't don't you *dare* blame me! Don't go there!

Master, Slinkbog is the one who's lying. I warned him about my boy and the carving, I did, I did, and now he's blaming you and—

No, no, no, Gnatsplat's the liar! He never told me anything. It was the ring, the ring. He should have told me he was bringing a ring.

No, a trillion times no, Slinkbog, you are a stupid, slimy slug with your sewage mouth—

—Shut up, you two. Just shut up and break up their engagement!

<hr>

The Fascinations of Murder

Tumbletwit,

It must have been satisfying for you, after working with your woman for so many years, to see her losing her wits during the media circus of sexual harassment accusations. But for us, beyond satisfying were the results of your perfect prompts as she tracked down the man she despised.

Yes, yes, yes, when he was let out on bail and went into hiding from reporters, I kept reminding her of all the things she knew about him. After their affair she'd obsessively monitored what he was doing and where he went, so last week I kept whispering, "You know how to find him, you know how to find him . . ." and all that thinking about tracking him down fired her up.

Oh, how it fired her up!

We saw that fire when she kicked open the door to his cabin with the gun in her hand. The moment she found him sitting at a table—

—Yes, that was the moment! I flooded her mind with infuriating things he'd done.

Up to that instant she'd only thought of threatening him. But with those enraging memories and her fury at the way he was denying everything, even laughing about the accusations—

—and so she squeezed the trigger . . . sending him into our hot, welcoming hands.

Well done, Tumbletwit!

Now everybody knows she fabricated her story of what happened. "We wrestled for the gun and it accidentally went off." Ha! They found five bullets in him.

Ha indeed! We've been watching her in the interrogations spinning and then respinning her tale. Most entertaining!

The best show of all is the media explosion. Millions of these human vermin are shooting at each other in their war of words. The press keeps whipping up both sides, quoting the most colorful zealots of either ilk shouting to "nail the extremists."

The extremists on the other side, of course. The contrasting posts are delightful—enough to make a stone gargoyle cackle.

"You have to believe this woman! That male monster is an abuser."

"Not so fast. She's a cold-blooded killer!"

Isn't it amazing, Tumbletwit, all we've accomplished in this culture?

Yes, yes, yes! Millions are politicizing guilt without having the foggiest notion of what really went on.

And isn't it fascinating how murder fascinates? Novels, movies, documentaries . . . thousands are killed on highways but murders get the attention. People know something crucial happened, but they're not sure what. They edge up to it with cop shows and horror films and murder mysteries.

Homicides rip off the masks disguising the moral stakes.

A Quaint Sexual Custom

Slinkbog,

You scatterbrained fumbler! Three months have gone by since that mission trip, and what have you done to break up this wedding juggernaut spreading havoc among us?

Have you used the local murder sensations to shake your girl?

Have you whispered obvious questions such as, "Why have all my prayers for my professor resulted in her killing a man?" You need a quiver-full of questions like that. Harden her heart.

And while luring her into useful emotions, subvert her commitment to save sex for marriage. Our decades of media dominance have created a culture that views celibacy before marriage as outdated and simply a silly, quaint sexual custom—but your girl won't budge on believing she should stay Miss Prissy till she's married.

Get to work! She's determined to wait, but she wants sex with her man. Whatever they do in his car or in the park, layer on guilt or disappointment or whatever presents itself.

These two are now, as the saying goes, "hot as pepper sprouts." Now is the time to sabotage their feelings that their romance is blessed by the celestials.

Plenty of effective, creative strategies are outlined in the *Brimstone Romantic Entanglements Guidebook*. Study it.

Use it to break them up.

Shrill Websites

Gnatsplat,

What are you doing with your Basement Boy? Is it really that hard to lure him with some click bait into the shrill websites he visited not long ago?

As I've repeatedly told you, make your boy despise the manacles of marriage. In those prenuptial sessions he's forced to sit through, have him see through the tripe about men loving and protecting their wives. Counter with whispers about nasty obligations and lost freedoms.

Use your man's clumsy ways with women and his sexual drives to push his fiancée far beyond her comfort zone. Get him amazed and exasperated at her reticence.

You and Slinkbog have a marriage to disrupt.

You are in very deep trouble if you don't.

A Sack of Temptations

Zitsit,

So you're alarmed at the threatening message you received from the lowerarchy: "Derail this wedding or else."

Or else what? You know very well.

Of course you're alarmed, and Gnatsplat and Slinkbog are just as terrified. You're all on the point, so get it done!

Your part is to stir up wedding tensions. Ignite your man's temper. Get him irritable and anxious. Have him make demands of his daughter and lure them into toxic disagreements so they lash out at each other.

Right now reach into your sack of temptations—you have plenty of them since he lives alone. Try:

Jealousy: stab him when he sees Gnatsplat's Basement Boy kiss his daughter.

Despair: crush him with the failures of the high school boys he works with and make him think his future son-in-law is just like them.

Doubt: flood him with it when he grieves his wife's death and wonders why the Enemy didn't heal her. Get him grumpy and angry about how he will be left alone as his daughter goes off to her married life.

Abort this wedding.

>10<

LOVE AND WAR

∧∧∧∧∧∧

"In every culture we generate hostility between the sexes."

∧∧∧∧∧∧∧

———

Nullifying Nuptials

Tumbletwit,

Good riddance to Gnatsplat, Slinkbog, and Zitsit. To use an apt curse from these human vermin, *May they rot in hell* . . .

Yesterday's insipid wedding ceremony ended our patience with those incompetent imps, and I'm told by the infernal powers, Tumbletwit, you are now on the point. You are to seduce both bride and groom.

We hate weddings. We hate even more marriages that grow out of ceremonies like the one that just caused us such disgust. All those flowers and promises and that sickness-and-health gush . . .

The lowerarchy will be scrambling some newbie imps to help you in your new assignment, but they'll likely be mere annoyances. You were selected for this post because you showed some spunk by finally getting a tight grip on your professor, reminding her of the graphic details of the seduction stories and keeping her breathing our oxygen till she pulled the trigger.

You did good work, Tumbletwit.

But don't expect free passes from me. No excuses, only results! You know the drill—break the bond between this man and this woman, and sever their connections with the cloying spirits who were everywhere at yesterday's ceremony.

We observed your glowering your way through it. We hope that means you were plotting to sabotage their commitments.

Get them off to a lousy start. During their first flicker of disagreement, remind them of what the bridesmaid read: "Love is patient and kind. Love is not jealous or proud or boastful or rude. Love does not demand its own way."

Whisper, "That's not how you're being treated by your spouse."

Whisper, "The ceremony lied. Turns out all these love claims are fantasy."

They believe they solemnly entered into something sacred. Pollute that! Make them believe marriage is just another transaction, like signing up for car payments. Convince them of our marriage mantra: "Promises made; things change. Move on."

Did you notice, at the phrase "till one shall lay the other in the arms of God," tears forming in the groom's eyes? Spin his maudlin feelings into fresh fears of marriage misery. Some day he's bound to wonder, "Did I make a mistake marrying this woman?"

Most important, get him out of his new love affair with the New Testament he's finding so unexpectedly fascinating.

Memorial Misery

Tumbletwit,

What's worse than a wedding like the one we endured a month ago? A memorial service of the same ilk.

Our exasperating Mrs. Gollyglowworm was eulogized in a service so bad it fit her nickname. What garbage! At eighty-nine, against all advice, she went tramping into the mountains far from medical help spreading rebellion and died alone on a dirt trail, but the speakers at her memorial transformed her stupidity into grand heroism.

Yes, they were absurd! And all those college students soaking it up made it misery to watch. Those heroic stories—

—and who, Tumbletwit, but your feisty bride and her brand-new husband were telling those stories? Your man stood by Gollyglowworm's casket describing the way her lantern was coming toward him as he was dying in the dark. Then his bride told how she'd bolted upright in bed. On and on they went about her inspiring them.

I know, I know, and I had tried everything to—

Not everything!

Right now they're on a double high of wedding and memorial service. That's the moment to catch them with their guards down. Your *Brimstone Guide* has countless temptations to dangle and clever lures to mess with their wills.

Have them ask themselves if their old anthropologist was heroic or reckless. Get them past heroism and deep into anxiety. It's everywhere in this culture.

Infect them with it.

Give these two a taste of dread.

Jail Jeopardy

Tumbletwit, you dolt, you dipstick . . .

. . . how could you possibly let your Miss Prissy—now your Mrs. Muck-it-up—decide she was going to visit our prey who is sitting stifled and barely sane in her cell? You've let your woman go way over the top—

—But, Master, these past weeks every time she saw a headline about the murder, and every time she read a posting about what should be done to her professor, she got more and more determined to visit her.

She kept pestering the chaplain's office and—

—And . . . so what? You let her go in there, and that's inexcusable. Why didn't you convince her to despise her murdering professor?

Oh, believe me, yes, that's exactly what I was doing over and over—and sometimes I would get a twinge of a response, but she kept shaking me off and praying about her own judgmental attitudes and for the woman "in need of redemption," so she got harder and harder to get through because those celestials kept hovering.

They followed her into the jail, and they soared over and around her as she walked into the cell—

—as they did when Miss Prissy walked into the professor's office with those same celestials. That time you were caught unawares, and once again—

—Oh, no, no, no! I saw this all coming and was doing everything I could to stop—

Really? We saw you swagger into her cell, shoving aside the jabbering imps the lowerarchy had sent in to taunt her. You should have been blocking your Mrs. Muck-it-up from ruining—

—But I wasn't swaggering, I was desperately trying to get into the professor's thoughts so that—

Why? She was no longer your client.

True, true, but since I was the one who had gotten her brain all scrambled and deadly, maybe I could get her angry at being invaded in her cell. But the instant I connected with her, something jack-hammered me into fragments of flashing colors and disorienting images. And those imps cowering in the corner—they weren't there because I shoved them, they were cringing at the light.

When my woman moved her hands onto the prisoner's head and started praying, her face was glowing—fearsomely glowing—and when she called out for heavenly forces, I was flattened.

I don't know what happened.

What did happen?

Tumbletwit, all I can tell you is that we are not at all pleased.

What's the Enemy up to? That's the question.

We know this—you must neutralize your newlywed crusader . . . and her now dangerous husband.

———

Male/Female Contempt

Tumbletwit, this is my last message to you . . .

. . . so study it carefully. I'm on to other seductions, but I'll leave you with a brief tutorial on tempting your bride and groom.

The Enemy has chosen to equip and energize these two, so the Brimstone strategy perfect for this couple is to shape their religious intensity into combative power plays.

Exploit their differences. For instance, during the wedding did you notice on the bride's face a slight ripple of puzzlement during "Amazing Grace" at the words, "How sweet the sound that saved a wretch like me"? Your woman doesn't think of herself as a wretch. She's never been a wretch like her new husband. His habits will exasperate her. You'll find plenty of angles for turning conversations into accusations.

She's a strong personality and deep down, so is he. Let the war begin. Draw your newlyweds from little discords down, down, down the ladder to dislike . . . distrust . . . disrespect . . . down to our prime marital condition of mutual contempt.

In every culture we generate hostility between the sexes.

Our Enemy created men to embrace and empower women. We seduce men to dominate and abuse women.

Our Enemy created women to join in holy alliances with men. We seduce women to unholy alliances of mutual disdain.

Never tolerate male/female harmony and mutual empowerment.

But, Devious Master, ever since these two agreed to devote themselves to prison ministry, they're tight as thieves. He's finding soul brothers among these men with bad experiences with their fathers, and when she visits women prisoners, she radiates hope. The women soak it up when she tells them they are beloved . . . and what can I do with those radiating celestials right in there with her?

Don't exaggerate—they're not always there. They come and go, and that's your opening for sowing doubts.

But right now those two have no doubts. All that spiritual energy in both of them—

Spiritual energy comes and goes, too. You know that from experience. Their own Scriptures say believers are mere "earthen pots" holding holy stuff.

Humans are full of chips and cracks and you need to wedge in your temptations of lust and pride—separating them from Enemy power.

To unpack my point, read bios of religious burnouts. Do your homework on couples we've successfully seduced and detoured into the most satisfactory of crimes and stupidities.

"Be perfect." That's what they're told to strive for, but they always fail at something. Stir up their failures into the usual bitterness and betrayals.

Use that brew to estrange them from the powers arrayed against us.

I repeat: never tolerate male/female harmony and mutual empowerment. Consider the history of the Mayo Clinic, an alarming illustration of the Enemy's mandate of man and woman empowering each other in his causes. The Mayo brothers pioneered medical advances. Nuns raised the money for a hospital. For decades women and men worked day and night together. Now we have branches of the Mayo Clinic all over the world with their "Faith, Hope and Science" motto—an extremely dangerous banner.

Think of it—"Faith, Hope and Science." Insidious!

Man/woman/faith/hope. That combination breaches our defenses. They empower these vermin against us. Think about Martin Luther marrying that nun who made possible so much of his miserable meddling.

I'm harping on all this because the woman now in your charge keeps drawing inspiration from William and Catherine Booth. You know full well how troubling that is. They marched together to a drumbeat that came directly from Enemy constellations. Now we've had more than a hundred years of the Salvation Army's disastrous intrusions.

And those damnable *bells* on the streets! As bad as churches ringing out hope!

Blunt the celestials' grip on your man and your woman by using every possible hook. Subvert all that love and redemption and forgiveness tripe they bought into at their wedding.

Above all, disconnect them from the Source of their faith. With celestials still hovering, who knows how this couple might assault our strongholds?

Remember this, Tumbletwit: We cannot and we will not tolerate another William and Catherine Booth!

END REFERENCES

We translators and editors, having worked so long extracting this story about a young man and woman, felt disappointed when we could find no further references in the messages to them. The East Orange download includes many more threads currently being translated, but none related to the newly married couple.

Our staff is still processing the experience of living with this project for nearly a year, wondering how the messages apply to the dramatic changes in our world. During our last editorial meeting, we discussed our concerns and decided to end this book with a few more carefully selected quotations.

We put up on a whiteboard dozens of staff-suggested quotes from a wide variety of sources, and then we whittled them down one by one to the nine you will find below.

The devil's finest trick is to persuade you that he does not exist.
—Charles Baudelaire

Satan disguises himself as an angel of light.
—2 Corinthians 11

<><><>

There are two great forces at work, God's force of good and the devil's force of evil. I believe Satan is alive and he is working, and he is working harder than ever, and we have many mysteries that we don't understand.

—Billy Graham

<><><>

The devil's most devilish when respectable.

—Elizabeth Barrett Browning

<><><>

Jesus knew that his hour had come to leave this world and return to his Father . . . It was time for supper, and the devil had already prompted Judas to betray Jesus.

—John 13

<><><>

Stand firm against the devil's strategies. We are not fighting against flesh-and-blood enemies, but against evil rulers and authorities of the unseen world, against mighty powers in this dark world, and against evil spirits in the heavenly places.

—Ephesians 6

<><><>

"Simon, Simon, Satan has asked to sift you like wheat. But I have prayed for you . . ."

—Jesus

<><><>

The devil hates us. He wants us to be as miserable as he is.

—Ezra Taft Benson

<>< ><>

Don't be a fool for the devil, darling.

—Anne Rice

www.ingramcontent.com/pod-product-compliance
Lightning Source LLC
Chambersburg PA
CBHW020023030726
47499CB00007B/2249